THE SECRETS WE BREAK

ONCE UPON A MURDER (BOOK 3)

SHERYL LISTER

SL BOOKS

ABOUT THE SECRETS WE BREAK

Gavin Black, the enigmatic owner of the town's most prestigious art gallery, is no stranger to secrets. When a high-profile figure who he's never gotten along with goes missing, Gavin finds himself under the scrutiny of law enforcement and the press. His carefully curated life begins to unravel when he's called in for questioning, casting a shadow over his reputation and his gallery.

Enter Nadia Dubois, an ambitious reporter with a nose for scandal, a heart of steel, and a knack for exposing the truth. Assigned to interview Gavin, Nadia sinks further into Gavin's world as she discovers an intricately layered charm that she didn't expect. With every revelation, their connection deepens, but so do the risks. And once Nadia unearths the dark truths hidden in the art world, she's torn between Gavin's allure and the secrets he guards so closely.

ISBN: 978-1-7373301-6-5

Design: Sherelle Green

ACKNOWLEDGMENTS

My Heavenly Father, thank you for my life and for loving me better than I can love myself.

To my husband, Lance, you will always be my #1 hero!

To my children, family and friends, thank you for your continued support. I appreciate and love you!

To my anthology sisters, you ladies are amazing!

Thank you to all the readers who have supported and encouraged me. I couldn't do this without you.

PROLOGUE

*G*avin Black Jr.'s hand stilled on the tie as he tried to block out the latest argument between his parents.

"This is only temporary, Gavin," he heard his mother say. "I'm sure we'll be back on our feet in no time."

"How? When? It's been over a year and we can barely keep this roof over our heads. We've lost everything thanks to those lies told by that damn Rivers family. And because they got the bank to manipulate my loan and ruin my credit in the process, we can't even get a loan for a light bulb. We can't get anything back, Vera. We don't have a house, jobs, and we barely have enough food for one person, let alone the five of us. We're living with your mother in this two-bedroom house with two growing boys. And what about Gavin? Do you know how it makes me feel to know we had to use his college fund to stay afloat? That ran out six months ago. Even if he gets a scholarship, he still needs food and clothes. Where is that money coming from? No one will even hire me. After all the money we spent trying to uplift this community and help everybody else, now that we need help, they're treating us like we have the plague!"

"Baby, I know. I'm going to go back and try to get more from the food bank after Gavin leaves for the college fair. There has to be a way."

"I don't want to talk about it anymore."

"Gavin—"

"Just go and leave me alone!"

Gavin's hands shook and tears filled his seventeen-year-old eyes as he continued to carefully knot the tie the way his father had shown him. He never knew life could be this hard. Last year, he had his own room in a four-bedroom house with enough food for two helpings at every meal. His clothes and shoes always fit and were new. Now, everywhere he went, people pointed, whispered and laughed behind his back, and some to his face. He couldn't remember the last time he'd had a full meal, the shoes he wore pinched his toes because he'd pretty much grown out of them, and his clothes were hand-me-downs from the church or thrift shop, including the suit he had on. The pants were at least two inches too short, but if he pulled them a little lower on his waist, it might not look so bad. And no one would know once his put on the jacket with its too short sleeves.

"You look so handsome, sweetheart," his mother said as she stood in the bathroom door.

"Thanks, Mom." She had a smile on her face, but Gavin could tell she'd been crying. Could see the pain and guilt in her eyes that she so valiantly tried to hide. She'd cried nearly every day over the past several months, though she had no idea he knew. He'd watched the life slowly leak out of her until there was nothing left of the vibrant woman who never failed to have a warm smile and kind word for everyone. Many days, Gavin watched her struggle to even get out of bed. He knew she was depressed. So was he. All because of greed. It wasn't enough that the Rivers had their own money.

They didn't want anyone else to have any, either. And he hated it. Hated *them*.

"Come on and get you something to eat before you go."

He followed her to the kitchen and took a seat in one of the old, scarred wooden chairs that wobbled, waiting while she dished up something from a small pot on the stove. "How's Grandma today?" The stress of losing the art gallery that had been in her family for two generations had been too much for Savannah Fleming, causing her to have a massive stroke.

"No change really. I don't think she'll be with us much longer," she added, her voice cracking.

His own emotions rose. Because they'd had no money and no insurance, the hospital refused to do anything more than stabilize her, even though the bulk of the cost for the updated facility had come from her family's wealth. Another reason he hated the Rivers family. She set a bowl in front of him half filled with some kind of broth. He spotted a few grains of rice and a couple of pieces of green beans. Today, there was no meat. It wasn't enough to quell the constant hunger pangs, but he didn't complain. It wouldn't do any good. Gavin scooped up a portion as his thirteen-year-old brother shuffled into the room and dropped down in the chair next to his. He scrutinized Micah for a moment. The weight loss was stark, his eyes almost hollow. His mother dished up another portion and set it in front of Micah. His brother said a quick blessing and dove in. The sight made his heart clench. Gavin ate a few more bites, then poured the rest into Micah's bowl. "I'm full, and I have to go." He quickly left the table before his mother could comment.

Half an hour later, he entered the high school gym crowded with other seniors hoping to snag one or more scholarships. With his portfolio of art, along with his transcripts, he headed straight for the table where two representatives from a West Coast art university sat. He introduced himself, answered their questions, and when requested, handed over his transcripts and a few samples of his artwork.

"These are very good, young man."

"Thank you."

"Did you get that suit from the thrift shop?"

Gavin froze when he heard the voice of the one person he had hoped to avoid. Monique Rivers.

"Of course you did. That's my daddy's old suit."

Monique laughed loudly and everyone in the gym turned their way. Gavin stood stoic as some of the students standing nearby snickered. He tried to ignore her, but she walked right up to the table as the two men sat with expressions of shock.

She grabbed the back collar of the suit coat and flipped it down. "See, it has his monogrammed initials. It doesn't even fit you," she taunted. "I can see a good two inches of your socks. Wait. Are those *holes* in your socks?" She threw her head back and laughed even harder, with some of the other students joining her.

Completely humiliated, he fought back the tears burning his eyes, mumbled an apology to the two men and ran out. Somehow, someway, he was going to get his family's money back and be richer than the Rivers family ever was, even if he had to work three jobs to do it. No one would ever laugh at him again.

CHAPTER 1

ENGAGING THE DEVIL

"*I* know that *bitch* didn't bring her ass up in here tonight!"

Gavin Black didn't bother to turn around, knowing full well who his brother meant. Only one woman could stir his younger brother's anger...hell, his entire family's anger if he were being honest. He took an unhurried glance over his shoulder and saw her moving through the art gallery like a participant on the red carpet. The people assembled watched her with expressions ranging from indifference and irritation to outright disgust. Gavin couldn't blame them. Monique Rivers and her family had been responsible for destroying many Black River Falls, South Carolina families. He turned back to his brother. "Ignore her, Micah," Gavin murmured. "All I want to do is make sure we sell well tonight." He'd held the summer art show yearly since opening Reflections Fine Art three years ago. However, this would be the first year that a portion of the sales would go toward art programs and scholarships for students.

Micah snagged a glass of wine from a passing waiter, still glaring at Monique. Despite their four-year age difference, with their similar height, build and looks, they'd often been mistaken for twins. "Whatever you say, big brother. I think I'm going to check out that collection of sculptures." He started off, then paused. "Great turnout, by the way."

"Thanks." It had taken him more than five years of hard work to bring his vision to fruition. Surveying the area, Gavin felt a deep sense of pride. Just as quickly, the old pain seared his heart. He caught Monique's gaze. She gave him a predatory smile and started his way. He smoothly pivoted on his heel and went in the opposite direction, not wanting to get into a confrontation with her because that's exactly what would happen if their paths crossed. Tonight, he only wanted to concentrate on successfully pulling off this event.

Gavin spent some time thanking everyone for coming, explaining pieces and encouraging them to purchase their favorites.

"Mr. Black, you're a hard man to reach."

He spun around at the sound of the sultry voice, and his gaze made a slow path from her stunning mocha-colored face, to her shapely curves in the body-hugging red minidress, down to her smooth, toned legs and feet in a pair of strappy sandals that matched her dress perfectly. Even in her heels, at six-four, Gavin still towered over her by a good seven or eight inches. "Am I? I can make myself available for the right person." He extended his hand. "And you are?" He knew a good number of the townsfolk, and definitely would've remembered her.

"Nadia Dubois," she said, placing her small hand in his and giving him a sensual smile. "Am I on your list of *right* people?"

Well now. Looks like the night just got more interesting. Gavin's brow lifted. "Depends on why you were trying to track me down."

Nadia laughed softly. "Officially, I'm a reporter for the

Black River Post and my first assignment is to interview you about the gallery and this fundraiser. Unofficially, maybe we can talk over coffee. I recently moved here and could use a tour guide."

A grin curved his lips. "I think I can accommodate you, *officially* and *unofficially*."

"Great." She pulled a business card and pen from her purse, wrote something on the back, then handed the card to him. "The front is for our official business. The number on the back is for...whatever else. Since I don't work weekends, I'll be back in the office on Monday."

The smile on her bronze-slicked lips sent a jolt to his groin. He was definitely down for all of it. "I'll call you then."

"Sounds good. I'm going to check out a few paintings."

"If you have any questions, let me know."

"I most certainly will, Mr. Black."

"Gavin."

She nodded. "Gavin it is."

Gavin's gaze followed her confident strut across the room. He liked a woman who knew who she was and what she wanted. Glancing down at the card, he noted her work hours, then flipped it over where she'd written her personal cell number. Smiling again, he stuck it in his breast pocket and headed toward a couple waving him over.

After answering their questions about the painting and artist, they purchased it and another one. He had his assistant, Leah Adams, handle the sale and arrange delivery. He meandered around the room, checking with the two artists who had pieces showing, and the catering staff to ensure they didn't need anything. Satisfied that everything was going according to plan, he picked up a toothpick holding a cherry tomato stuffed with mozzarella and popped it into his mouth. Gavin disposed of the toothpick in the provided mini trash bowl.

"What's up, Professor?"

He shook his head at the high school nickname he'd been given while playing football because he always had to have a strategy for every play. He greeted Sinceer, Khalil and Knox. "I appreciate you guys stopping by." Of all the guys on the team, these three were the only ones he hung out with because they'd been there for him during the dark times of his life.

"There's some cool shit in here," Sinceer said.

Khalil nodded. "Maybe I need to have you do a commissioned piece."

"Whenever you're ready, let me know. I'd be happy to do pieces for all of you." Gavin studied Knox. He had always been the nice guy and the quietest of the bunch. "You good, Knox?"

"Yeah. But I'm going to take off. I just wanted to stop in."

"It's all good." After watching Knox weave through the crowd and to the exit, he turned back to the other two men. "Take a look around and enjoy the food and wine." He spoke with them a moment longer before Sinceer and Khalil headed over to get drinks.

Gavin continued making rounds, but he never lost sight of Nadia. Each time their gazes connected, she smiled, teasing, taunting as they moved throughout the space in a sensual dance. A while later, he spotted her studying one of his paintings and went to join her, standing behind her and slightly to her left. He stuck his hands in his pants pockets and observed as she angled her head one way, then another.

Finally, Nadia said, "I'm trying to figure out how you did this on three different canvases, yet it's as if each one merges into the other like one complete picture."

"It is one picture, and they're called multi-panel pieces."

"But, how?"

"Each artist has their own process, but I typically tape the canvases together before painting, then take them apart after they've dried."

She faced him. "I never would've thought to do that. But then I can't even make stick figures look good."

He laughed. "I'd be more than happy to teach you a few things. I mean, you did say I could call you for…whatever."

"Hmm, I did. And you think you can show me how to do a decent landscape like this one? Of course, mine would need to be far less complex." She waved a hand toward the picture. "Like no trees, shadows, moon half covered, clouds, distant mountains…"

"So what exactly would be on this painting?"

Nadia made a show of thinking, then her face lit up. "Ooh, I know. A sky and some water."

She totally captivated him, and he loved her energy. "I believe I can handle that. Let me know when you're ready to start your lessons."

"I'll do that. But for now, I want to purchase this one. The purple and black sky with the fat moon partially hidden is so hauntingly beautiful. It makes me feel…I don't know. It just speaks to me."

It was always his hope that every one of his creations— paintings or sculptures—would evoke some type of feelings, and her words touched the artist in him. "Thank you." Rather than have his assistant handle the sale, he did it himself, and promised to have it delivered to her on Monday. She thanked him and said her goodbyes.

An hour later, only two or three people remained as the fundraiser came to an end. His ever-efficient assistant hurried them along and they closed the door on the last one shortly after. Or so he thought. He stepped back into the gallery and froze. "What the hell are you still doing here, Monique? We're closed."

She didn't say anything for a moment, but stared at a

painting as if she was interested in it. Turning his way, she smiled brightly and sauntered in his direction, stopping within inches of him. "I was thinking about the last time we were alone in a gallery together. The kiss we shared."

"Obviously, we don't have the same recollection." That incident had happened several years ago when he was celebrating his first major commissioned piece and he'd had way too much to drink, but he wasn't drunk enough to hop into bed with the wife of one of his friends. And especially not her.

"I didn't want your ass anyway. I just needed information to get my hands on that gallery for my daddy," Monique tossed out. She looked him up and down. "You weren't even good for that."

Gavin felt the old rage rising. "You need to leave."

"You're not fooling me, Gavin. I *know* you want me. You always did."

"You're delusional," he said with a bitter chuckle. She'd cost his family *everything* and tried to humiliate him. He wouldn't want her if she was the only woman left in the galaxy.

She turned a slow circle. "This is a nice place. *Small*, but nice. It's too bad your father couldn't make that payment back then." Fingering the lapel on his suit coat, she said, "At least you have clothes that fit you now. And the buffet earlier was a nice touch. You probably could've used that back when your family was standing in the free food line."

He pushed her hand aside, latched on to her arm, and marched her over to the door. "Get out."

"Take your hand off me!" She snatched away, pure hatred blazing in her eyes. "Don't forget, I can *break* you!"

"Give it your best shot because you'll only get one," he said with lethal calmness.

She stormed past him, her shoulder purposely brushing his chest.

"One more thing. I'm not my father." He slammed the door behind her, turned the lock and tried to rein in his anger.

Ms. Leah came around the corner and shook her head. "Ugh! I can't stand that heffa." She waved a hand. "But I don't want to talk about her. I want to celebrate tonight. Gavin, this was a *brilliant* idea. We always do pretty well, but adding the fundraiser for kids had people digging a little deeper into their pockets. I'll tally up the sales, and prepare the artist commissions on Monday." They walked to the back leading to the offices and stopped at hers.

"I appreciate all your hard work, Ms. Leah." She was closer to his mother's age and had been a godsend to him and his family. They all considered her one of them. "You can go on home and I'll lock up. I may stay a while longer to work on a couple of things." His art calmed him.

"Okay, if you're sure." Ms. Leah lifted one foot, took off her shoe, then did the same with the other. "I don't know how women walk around all day in these heels. My feet are killing me." She dropped them into her tote and replaced them with a pair of flat shoes. "Ah, that's better."

Shaking his head at her humor, he waited until she gathered her belongings, then walked her out the rear door to her car, threw up a wave and went back inside and to the front to secure everything and turn off the lights. Now that the adrenaline of the night had worn off, fatigue hit him. He'd spent at least twelve hours at the gallery every day for the past two weeks, including weekends, to make sure the evening would go off without a hitch. He'd planned to go home and crash, but now with all the anger swirling in his belly, he needed to find his center. He just hoped Monique heeded his warning.

Three days later...

BREAKING NEWS
Monique Rivers, Daughter of the Late Humphrey Rivers, Missing.
Foul Play Suspected.

CHAPTER 2

*S*unday afternoon, Nadia rushed down the hallway to her bedroom to catch her ringing phone. A smile curved her lips when she saw her best friend's name on the display. "Well if it isn't the world traveler. Hey, girl. Are you guys back?" She dropped down on the bed.

Laughter came through the line. "Yes, and it was absolutely *amazing*. A month of rest, relaxation, and my hubby's undivided attention...pure heaven."

"You know I'm so jealous right now," she said with a chuckle. She and Brooklyn Hall had been friends since middle school. They'd weathered puberty, first loves and heartbreak together and were as close as sisters. "Speaking of Vince, how is he?"

"He was with me, how do you think he's doing? Let's just say, a few of those excursions we'd planned got canceled. All those sexy outfits we found were put to very good use."

They screamed with laughter. "I can't with you, girl." She figured by now, at age thirty-six, she'd be married with maybe one or two kids, and for sure having getaways with the love of her life. But that's not how life turned out for her.

"You are too bold." Although, Nadia had been a little bold herself last night at the gallery.

"Hey, I'm just trying to keep the marriage sexy and exciting. And you know I've always gone after what and *who* I wanted. Okay, enough about me. What the hell happened at the paper? When I left, you'd just finished a great story, then I got your email talking about you'd been fired and were moving."

She let out a deep sigh. "The story exposed some fraud at a company owned by one of Ronnie's friends. When I wouldn't give up my source, he gave me an ultimatum— name my source or resign. I chose to keep my integrity." Her boss had hounded her for a good three weeks to name the whistleblower who'd disclosed that a CEO at one of the tech industry giants was using corporate funds as his personal piggy bank. Nadia wouldn't budge on her position, and he made good on his threat.

"You have got to be kidding me. That asshole. It wouldn't surprise me if he's doing something shady, too."

"I agree, and the thought did cross my mind. It was pretty hypocritical and self-serving considering he preached confidentiality on a daily basis. But that wasn't the worst part."

"Hold on. I feel like I'm gonna need wine for this."

"Maybe I should pour myself a glass, too."

"Uh oh. What?"

"He tried to get Austin to pressure me. You remember he and Ronnie went to college together."

"As in Austin, your ex?"

"Yeah. I hadn't talked to him since showing him the door a year ago, and he had the nerve to try to tell me that my integrity meant nothing without a job. It took every ounce of control I had not to punch him in his face, especially since he can't spell integrity, let alone question someone else's." They'd dated for almost three years with him making one promise after another of marriage and children, until she found out he'd made that same promise to two other women.

"Un-freakin-believable! I don't know if I would've had your restraint, sis. Okay, I get all that, but why the big move all the way across the country? And to a small town that seems to be a little strange. Not gonna lie, I was kind of upset to get back and find my bestie gone."

A small measure of guilt surfaced. "I know, and I'm sorry. I thought I could put it all behind me after I left the job, but the harassment didn't stop, so I left. I wanted to wait until you came back, but my condo sold in less than a week and I got offered a job at the paper here. It seemed like a sign." She would miss living in Seattle and being able to see her parents and friends, but her peace and sanity outweighed everything. Except that peace had been invaded already. Austin and Ronnie had texted her the first week after her move citing all the reasons why she should reconsider. She'd blocked both their numbers.

"Yeah, I guess. I know your parents were sad to see you leave."

"You can always come and visit me. And yes, they were. But Dad told me I needed to do what made me happy." He'd also told her he was proud of her for standing up to the bullying.

"As soon as I'm rested, I will. What do you think of Black River Falls so far? Is it as mysterious as some people say? And are there any fine men?"

"How did I know that would be on your list of questions? I've only been here two weeks, and with getting moved in and adjusting to a new job, I haven't really had a chance to explore. I did get my first assignment to interview the owner and manager of one of the art galleries." Gavin's handsome face floated through her mind.

"That seems like a step down with all your experience."

"I thought so, too, until I met the owner...well over six feet, rich chocolate skin, dark, cinnamon eyes, and fine as hell." There was something about those eyes—with a color that fell somewhere between light and dark—that exuded a warmth and drew her in the moment they met.

"What's his name?"

"Gavin Black. And there isn't one thing *strange* about him. I went to the fundraiser event last night and one look at him had me channeling you. I gave him my card, told him he could call me for the interview, wrote my number on the back, and said he could call me for whatever."

There was silence for several seconds, before Brooklyn screamed with excitement. "*Whaaaat?* I can't believe it. What did he say?"

"He said he could accommodate me *officially* and *unofficially.*"

"Oh, hell yeah. I'm definitely going to have to make a trip. After all these years, you finally made the first move. I'm so proud."

Smiling, Nadia said, "Shut up."

She burst out laughing. "Seriously, though I'm happy for you and I hope he turns out to be the one for you. You deserve someone special."

"We'll see. I just met the man less than twenty-four hours ago and I can't think of doing anything until I do the interview." She didn't even want to think about how it would look if she started dating him before finishing her first assignment. She'd just lost one job and couldn't afford to lose another one.

"Yeah, I see your point. But after your business is done... Does he just own it or is he an artist, as well?"

"Both. And oh, my goodness, he has incredible talent. I went just to meet him and see the gallery and ended up buying a landscape painting. My mouth dropped when I realized it was one of his."

"That's cool. I've never met an artist. Hmm, I wonder if all that creativity extends to other areas of his life. Ooh, I'm going to send you the links to a few of the sexy lingerie I bought. You need to upgrade your bedroom wardrobe. Do they even have a mall?"

"Again, I have no idea. But I'm sure there are places to shop since ain't nobody walking around butt naked."

"Whatever."

Nadia heard Vince say something to Brooklyn. "Tell him I said hello."

"I will. I need to go. We're having Sunday dinner with his parents and you know my mother-in-law doesn't like folks to be late to her table."

"I remember." Nadia had met the woman at a few gatherings and she was a stickler for punctuality. "Have fun."

"I'm going to have a good time eating, that's for sure. We'll talk soon. Keep me updated on your artist and text me a picture of him so I can check him out."

"I'll send it when I hang up." She hadn't been able to resist getting a shot of him. They said their goodbyes and she disconnected, then sent the picture. Her phone chimed less than a minute later and she read her friend's reply: *I'm definitely sending those links because that man is fine, fine, FINE!*

Nadia burst out laughing at the row of fire emojis. "Crazy woman," she mumbled and tossed the phone aside. Speaking of food, she needed to figure out what to have for her own dinner. It was almost six and she'd been so busy cleaning and unpacking boxes, she'd skipped lunch. She probably should make another trip to the grocery store, but the summer heat and humidity made her want to stay inside instead. Rising to her feet, she headed toward the kitchen, but stopped when her phone chimed again.

Nadia frowned. She didn't recognize the number and her thumb hovered over the delete button for a brief moment, wondering if her ex was messaging her from a different number, before deciding to open the text. She relaxed when she realized it was from Gavin: *Just wanted you to have my number in case you needed anything. I did agree to be your tour guide.*

Nadia: *Thanks. Any good food places I should try?*

Gavin: *If you like soul food and ribs, Uncaged Soul is the place to go. I'd be more than happy to take you.*

As much as she wanted to say yes, she should wait until she finished the interview. Nadia: *Maybe after our official business is done.*

Gavin: *I can go with that. Tomorrow. Your office or mine. The quicker we get that business done, the faster we can do...whatever.*

Her pulse skipped. The brother was smooth.

I can go with that, she texted, throwing his words back. Then added, *Your office at 10.*

A smile played around the corner of her mouth. She hoped Brooklyn sent those links soon.

"Gavin, there's someone here to see you."

Gavin spun around and glanced up at the wall clock. He'd lost track of time working on a new piece and it was time for his meeting with Nadia. "Tell her I'll be out in a minute."

Ms. Leah clucked her tongue. "You really should set an alarm when you start creating. You forget everything when you get in this studio."

He grinned sheepishly. She'd been saying the same thing for more than two decades and often brought him food. Otherwise, he would've skipped eating for hours. "I know. I had planned to, but—"

"But you went straight for the canvas and forgot. Again."

Gavin held his hands up in mock surrender and laughed. "You win. I'm going to clean up. Give me three minutes before bringing Nadia in my office."

She eyed him critically. "Take five. I saw the two of you on Friday night. Oh, and spray on a little of that cologne I know you keep hidden in the back of your desk drawer," she added and sailed out.

His mouth fell open and he couldn't stop the laughter that poured out of him. She had always been a bright spot, particularly during those times when he'd had little to smile about. Pushing aside the dark memories, he headed to his office to clean up.

Gavin stripped off the paint-splattered T-shirt, went into the private bathroom he'd added and washed up. He learned early on to keep a stash of shirts, slacks and sport coats just in case for business purposes. After changing into black slacks and mint green button-down silk shirt, he stepped into his loafers and headed out to meet Nadia. Thinking about what Ms. Leah said, he turned back, sat in his chair and reached for the bottle of cologne tucked away. After spraying a little, he chuckled and replaced it in the drawer. His head came up when he heard the knock. Coming to his feet, he met Nadia's gaze. Today, she wore a pair of cream-colored slacks with a bright tangerine sleeveless top that dipped in the front, giving him a glimpse of her full breasts. "Ms. Dubois, nice to see you again. Please come in and have a seat." He gestured to the chair across from his desk. "Thanks, Ms. Leah."

"You're welcome. I see you took my advice." She tossed him a wink and closed the door.

Nadia sat and crossed her legs. "I like her. She reminds me a little of my mother."

"She's the best." Gavin rounded the desk and reclaimed his chair. "So, did you find a spot to eat last night?"

"I decided to stay in." Staring directly at him, she added, "And save that soul food for another time." She cleared her throat. "I know you're busy, so we can get started. Would it be okay if I recorded our interview?" She must have seen the wary look in his eyes because she quickly said, "It's only for me to make sure I don't miss anything. As soon as the article is done, I'll erase it. I promise. I'm very serious about confidentiality."

Something in her tone gave him pause, as did the quick flash of anger in her eyes. He wondered why. Had someone invaded her privacy? Admittedly, he'd had second and third thoughts about doing the interview. The thought of his face being splashed across the newspaper again brought up heartbreaking memories he'd rather leave behind. Gavin refused to have his family subjected to the same scrutiny that had dogged them for almost two years. He'd give her all the information she needed as it related to the gallery and his art, but his family and personal life was strictly off limits. "That's fine."

Nadia set the small recorder on the desk. "Let's start with how you got into art."

He smiled. "My grandmother was a gifted artist and I loved watching her create amazing sculptures from lumps of clay, vivid sunrises and sunsets on blank canvases and intricate layers of color in plain glass dipped in fire. Every summer, I spent hours with her in the studio."

"That had to be an incredible experience."

"It was. Although, it often got me into trouble when I skipped out on my chores."

She laughed softly. "I can imagine. Your grandmother must have been very patient."

"She had the patience of a saint. I probably asked at least a hundred questions every single day." His mind drifted to those times. *"Grandma, why are you using that kind of paint? What happens if you leave the clay in the kiln too long? Can I try to make the clay pot this time?"* Vera Fleming had taught him, gently corrected him, and never criticized the art he created. She often said, *"There's no wrong in art. Everyone interprets it differently."* He came back to the present when Nadia asked him another question.

"Is she still alive?"

Pain settled in his heart. "No," he said softly. "She passed away over twenty years ago."

"I'm sorry, Gavin. I wish I could've met such an extraordinary woman." She fell silent, as if she sensed he needed a moment. "Do you have any other family members who are artists?"

"My mother used to paint some, but she stopped several years ago. I have a cousin who sculpted, but she's out of the business, as well." Giselle had disappeared two decades ago and, after searching for years, his family had given up hope that they'd ever see her again. He also blamed the Rivers for that.

"It's great to see you carrying on the family legacy." Then she continued asking about his education and how he decided on art as a career.

"I went to the Academy of Art University in San Francisco and was fortunate enough to study abroad in Florence for a summer. Then I got my MBA from USC." Once again, the darkness of those times tried to pull him under. Had it not been for scholarships, he would've never been able to attend any college. Gavin studied harder, worked harder because he knew he was the way up for his family.

"That's amazing. Tell me more about your studies in Florence."

"They had a partnership with an international art

program, and for seven weeks, I was able to study and create art under some of the best instructors. We also had an opportunity to explore Tuscany." He would never forget Professor Arison, who made it possible for Gavin to have one of best experiences of his life. As a result, Gavin had art contacts in Italy and a few other countries, as well as here in the States. The professor had retired years ago, but Gavin still kept in touch with the man.

"Wow. Based on the pieces I've seen, I think you mastered those studies."

"Thanks. But there's always something to learn."

She nodded. "Never stop learning, right?"

"Something like that."

"What are your favorite mediums to work with?"

"Clay, acrylics and oils for painting, and glass are my favorites, but I experiment with other mediums as well."

"Such as?"

He angled his head and thought for a moment. "I've done a few things with watercolors, oil pastels and some mixed media pieces."

Her brows knitted together. "Can you elaborate on mixed media?"

"Sure. It's a type of visual art that combines more than one medium or material. An example would be using paint, paper, and fabric together, sort of like a collage. There's also something called assemblage, and it's a 3-D version of a collage and could include elements that stick out from the background."

"I'd love to see that if you have them available."

"I think there are a couple of pieces in the gallery done by another artist. We can take a look after we're done."

"Sounds good. Would it be okay if I took a few photos to showcase?"

Gavin nodded.

Nadia looked down at the notebook that she'd been writing in and flipped back and forth for a moment. "I know the fundraiser was for scholarships and art programs. Tell me more about your vision."

"There are quite a few talented students in town, but just like every other school district, there isn't much funding when it comes to the arts. I want those who wish to pursue it as a career to have options. Also, I hold an eight-week teen summer program on Thursdays for two hours from eleven to one." It took him only one week to find out that getting up early in the summer wasn't on the any of the student's lists, and they did better with the later time. "My goal is to hire a couple of art instructors and expand the summer program to include elementary and middle schoolers."

"The students here are fortunate to have someone like you in their corner." She wrote something else. "Now, in anticipation of our interview, I did a little research on your family's history in the art world and saw that you used to own the Riverwood Gallery, which is now owned by..." She glanced down at her notes. "The Rivers family. Can you shed some light on what happened?"

His jaw tightened. "My family's history is off limits."

Nadia flinched. "I see. Do you think you might share the story with me sometime in the future, off the record?"

He hadn't meant to snap at her, and he couldn't fault her for doing her job. Trying to soften his words, he said, "Maybe. We'll see." He rotated his chair and stared out the window.

"Then we'll leave it." They talked for another fifteen minutes. "I think that's about all I have, unless there's something else you'd like to share."

"I don't have anything else."

Nadia clicked off the recorder, stuffed it and her notebook and pen into a tote before coming to her feet. "I really appreciate you taking time to talk to me. I want you to know that I don't sensationalize my articles. I'm a journalist who takes the facts and presents them in an interesting way. I'll let you read it before I turn it in."

Gavin came to his feet. "I appreciate that, and I apologize for my abrupt answer earlier."

She waved him off. "We all have things in our past that haunt us, and it's obvious that you're very protective of your family. I can't be upset about that. In fact, I think it's an admirable trait."

He studied her, looking for any hint of deceit, but only saw genuine compassion. Several other reporters had wanted to do stories on the gallery and his family over the years, but none had shown the sensitivity Nadia had, resulting in a standard "no comment" to every question. But this newcomer was different, and in a good way. "Come on. I'll show you the mixed media pieces and you can take your pictures." He opened the door and gestured her forward.

As they walked toward the showroom, Nadia said, "As soon as this article is printed, I'll be looking to collect on that soul food dinner." She pointed a finger his way. "And after the way you made my mouth water, it better be as good as advertised."

Gavin laughed. "It will be. I promise." Nadia's vibrant personality had him laughing and smiling more than he had in the past two years. He couldn't wait until the article was published. *I'll be ready for whatever and more.*

CHAPTER 3

THE INTERROGATION

BREAKING NEWS

*Renowned Artist and Gallery Owner Brought in for Questioning
in Relation to Vanished Mogul.*

"You all didn't have to come to the airport," Gavin said to his five Los Angeles cousins. "Especially since it's so early on a Sunday morning." They were the children of his father's younger brother and they'd had a close relationship as kids. But when he was twelve, his father had packed the family up and moved from LA to Black River Falls where his mother's family had roots. The brothers had had some kind of falling out and hadn't spoken since then. Gavin's father would never give the reason, and Gavin had asked many times over the years.

Nicholas, the oldest at thirty-eight, laid a hand on Gavin's shoulder. "Man, you're our cousin and we miss you and

Micah. We know our fathers have some issues, but that has nothing to do with us."

"Exactly. We don't need to get involved their shit," Marcel said. At third oldest, he stood a couple of inches taller than Gavin and was ex-military. "We were pissed when we heard about what happened to y'all with those crazy ass people and wish we could've helped."

Gavin didn't want to rehash old history. "It's okay. We're good now. I really like BlackLux and I'll definitely be back to visit," he said, changing the subject. The siblings had recently opened an upscale bar and entertainment venue. "I'm going to try to convince Micah to come with me next time." Reconnecting with his family had been good and he was glad he finally took them up on their offer to visit, even if only for a weekend. "I'd better go." He shared rough hugs with his four male cousins. Alana, the only girl gave him a strong hug.

"I'm so glad to finally meet you, Gavin," she said. "Don't be a stranger. Oh, I love art, so I'll be planning a trip to visit."

"That sounds good." She and her twin brother Zaire had just been born when they moved and he'd never even had a chance to see them.

Up to this point, Raheem remained silent. "Tell Micah I'll be waiting to kick his butt on the court."

He smiled. "I'll do that." Raheem and Micah were the same age and had been joined at the hip, and spent many days on the basketball court together. Knowing he had to get moving, he said, "I'll be in touch soon. It was good to see you again." After a final round of goodbyes, he headed to the security checkpoint.

An hour later, Gavin settled in his airplane seat. As much as he'd enjoyed the visit, he wanted to get back home. It had been almost a month since the interview and, outside of texts, phone calls, and one meet up at the bakery for coffee, he and Nadia still hadn't gotten that dinner due to both of their schedules. True to her word, she'd sent him a copy of her article and he'd been impressed by her professionalism and objectivity. The story had run a couple of weeks ago and, as a result, he'd seen an increase in foot traffic. He'd have to thank her. His cell rang, reminding him that he hadn't put it on airplane mode. He saw his brother's name on the display and connected.

"Hey, baby bro."

"How was the visit?"

"It was great to see them. Raheem said he'll be waiting to kick your butt on the court."

Micah snorted. "In his dreams." He paused. "Maybe I'll go with you next time."

"Sounds good. The plane is getting ready to leave, so we'll talk when I get home."

"Later."

He disconnected, switched the mode and stuck the phone back in his pocket. Leaning back, he closed his eyes. He understood Micah's hesitation. After being out of their lives for so long, he'd been apprehensive about how their cousins, aunt and uncle would behave. So had Gavin, if he were being truthful. However, they'd embraced him and treated him as if that time never existed. Gavin really wished he knew what caused the rift. His Uncle Nick had pulled Gavin aside and questioned him about Gavin, Sr. He told him to relay the message that his door would always be open for a reconciliation. It made Gavin speculate that whatever had happened was on his father's part.

He spent the flights going over his schedule for the upcoming week and contemplating his next pieces. By the time he landed, he'd sketched out three sculptures. After placing the pad he never left home without into his messenger bag, he deplaned and headed for the exit.

"Mr. Black, you're a hard man to reach."

Gavin turned and saw Nadia. She'd said the same thing that first night. "Hey. What are you doing here? Leaving or returning?"

"Just getting back from visiting my parents in Seattle. Business trip?"

"Nah. Spending time with my family in LA. Is that where you're from?"

"Yes. You know I'm still waiting on that dinner, the *whatever* and anything else."

Grinning, he and shook his head. "Hey, I'm not the only one who's been busy."

"We're not talking about me," Nadia said with a straight face, then burst out laughing.

"No time like the present to kick things off, unless you have something planned for the evening."

A smile lit her face. "I have laundry planned." She made a show of thinking. "Let me see...dinner with you or laundry. It's a tough choice, but I'll take dinner."

"Thanks. I think. Can't say I've ever had a woman have to think hard about having dinner with me or doing laundry."

"Aw, I was just playin'." She leaned closer and whispered, "I'll let you in on a little secret. I *hate* doing laundry, but don't tell my mother. She believes laundry should be done every single week without fail. Me, I wash when I don't have a choice." She shuddered.

Laughing, Gavin said, "Your secret is safe with me. You want that soul food or something else?"

"Could we get something to go this time? After traveling all day, I just want to put my feet up. And I completely forgot about having to drive from Charleston to Black River Falls."

"Did you drive?"

"I rented a car and planned to rent another one for the ride home."

Her not having a car would give them more time

together. "My car is in the lot, so you don't need to rent a car. Do you have any other bags to get?"

"Nope. I just have this one. And thanks. I can give you gas money."

Gavin gave her a sidelong glance. "If you pull any money out of your purse, I'm going to be offended, and I really don't want us to start off on the wrong foot."

Nadia raised a hand in mock surrender. "Say no more. Me and my purse are just going to sit quietly. Let me cancel my rental real quick." She made a call and then dropped her phone in her purse.

"You are something else." He'd never met a woman quite like her. They went to the lot and he led her to his car.

"Nice ride," she said of his late model Mercedes.

"Thanks." He'd promised himself one item of luxury once he got his family back on their feet. Gavin had made good on both. He stashed their bags, helped her in, then climbed in on the driver's side. They rode the first few minutes in companionable silence. Since she mentioned Seattle being home, he was curious as to why she would leave a large, robust city for their little dark corner of the state. "You mentioned you were from Seattle. What made you move here?"

For a moment, she said nothing, just stared out the window.

"I'm sorry if I'm prying."

"No, it's okay. I left because I needed a change."

"Black River Falls isn't exactly the place where people tend to relocate, particularly with your journalistic experience."

"I was forced to resign from my last job because I published an article about a CEO who was using company funds for personal use. The guy happened to be friends with my immediate supervisor, but he couldn't stop the story from running because the chief and managing editors approved it and were eager to break the news before some other newspaper. He started harassing me about my source and gave me an ultimatum—give up my source or resign." Nadia shifted in her seat and looked his way. "You can guess which option I chose."

"That's ridiculous. Aren't there laws to protect sources?"

"Yep. But that didn't stop him. He made my life a living hell, even after I quit." She paused. "Then he tried to get my ex to bully me out of the information."

Gavin whipped his head in her direction, then back to the road, jerking back into his lane. "You have got to be kidding me."

"I wish I was. I started applying for positions at other papers, but Ronnie pretty much had me blackballed."

"I'd think papers would want someone with your integrity."

"You'd think, but apparently not enough to hire me. I came to South Carolina to get away for a few days and started looking into jobs. I took the first offer, put my condo on the market, packed up and left."

He found himself getting angry and wished he could have five minutes with both men. When Gavin got done with them, they'd think twice before harassing her or any other woman. "Have they tried contacting you since you moved here?"

"Yes. I blocked their numbers, though. I thought about changing my number, but I didn't want to go through the hassle of contacting every single person I know."

"If they call you again, let me know. I have a friend who works for the sheriff's department."

"Thanks. I'll do that."

As he drove, he found out that Nadia was an only child, but had a best friend who doubled as a sister, had degrees in journalism and communication, and had contemplated applying for a position as a foreign correspondent. "So, when you're not working, what do you like to do?"

"Not painting, that's for sure."

Gavin threw his back and roared with laughter.

Joining in his laughter, she said, "Hey, I know how to stay in my lane. I actually like reading and would love to write a romance or thriller someday."

"After reading the piece you did on the gallery, I could see you doing something like that. You could end up on one of those bestseller lists and have your book turned into a movie." Her captivating writing would certainly garner attention.

"I've never thought about that. Hmm...that's a great idea. I need to start getting those plot bunnies working. Now, it's your turn. Tell me a little bit about your town. I heard a rumor that Phantom Lake is haunted and that one man found dead bodies of newcomers who didn't believe."

"Old Man Chandler said he found them while he was fishing. Not sure why he was fishing in that lake, but I wouldn't even think about eating those fish and be the next one to die."

"You believe it?"

"Since I never saw those people again, yes. Of course, they could've moved away, but to disappear suddenly...I don't think so."

"That's fascinating. Not the people disappearing," she corrected quickly, "but just the mystery of it all from a journalistic perspective."

"I know what you meant."

"This is a nice town. Quaint and the lake is beautiful."

"Rosewood Heights is a little larger than our town and most folks prefer not to be associated with what they believed was *haunted land.*"

"Hmm, interesting. I never knew small towns had such

intrigue. Whenever people talk about them, all I hear is charming and sweet."

Those words could never be used to describe his hometown, and he wondered if there ever was a time when they did apply. As they crossed the Elm Street Bridge that connected Rosewood Heights to Black River Falls, he asked, "Have you decided what you want to eat? We can take it back to my place or yours, whichever you prefer."

"I want to try the soul food, and let's go to your place. I'm curious about where you live."

Gavin drove to Uncaged Soul. He spotted Sinceer at the bar, but he appeared to be busy, so he sent a nod his way instead. He and Nadia grabbed menus and, after she spent several minutes going back and forth between the Jail Break seafood plate and the Prison Plate with ribs and soul food sides, she chose the latter. He paid for their dinners and they headed to his house.

"*This* is your house?" Nadia asked as he pulled into the driveway minutes later. "It's beautiful."

"Thanks." He'd purchased the four-bedroom, four-bath ranch-style house because it reminded him of the one he'd grown up in until it was snatched from them. "Do you need anything out of your bag? If not, we can leave it in the car."

"We can leave it."

They walked up the four steps that led to a porch that spanned the entire front of the house.

Nadia looked up at him. "If I lived here, you'd have to pry me off this porch. That swing would be my happy place."

"We can sit out here for a while after we eat if you'd like. And you can stop by whenever to use it." *Where the hell did that come from?* He'd never given any woman the freedom to invade his privacy. Yet, it didn't bother him as much as it should have.

"Ooh, I like." She wiggled her eyebrows and rubbed her

hands together. "Hopefully, the summer heat will have gone down some."

"Maybe. If not, I'll turn on the fans." He pointed to the ceiling.

"Yep, you're going to have to drag me out kicking and screaming. My little two-bedroom rental barely has a front yard and the porch is only wide enough for two people to walk side-by-side to the front door."

Gavin unlocked the door and stepped back so she could go first.

"I'm definitely going to have to find something like this when I decide to buy a house," she murmured as she entered the foyer. After toeing off her shoes, she padded barefoot to the living room. "Were you married before? Have a couple of kids stashed somewhere? And how old are you anyway?"

Going down the short hallway leading to the kitchen, he chuckled and waited for her to follow. "No, no, and I just turned forty. And you?"

"No, I wish, and thirty-six."

With her experience, he figured she had to be somewhere in her thirties, though she looked far younger. And she wished for children, something that hadn't ever been on his radar because he never believed he'd let anyone get close to his heart to have that kind of relationship. After they washed their hands, he unloaded their meals and went to the cabinets for plates, serving spoons and silverware. They'd both gotten The Prison Plate, which included a half slab of ribs, greens, sweet potatoes, cornbread, and mac and cheese. Sinceer had done time in the past and had given the various plates on his menu prison names.

Nadia came around the bar to where he stood opening the containers. "Mmm, it smells so good." She snagged a stray piece of meat, then licked the sauce off her fingers. Her eyes slid closed, and she let out a soft moan.

The sound sent a jolt straight to his groin.

"I think you might be right about this food, and I can't wait to dig in."

"You're welcome. You have a little sauce on your chin." He reached over and wiped it off with the pad of his thumb. For a charged moment, they just stared at each other. He moved closer and dipped his head, then pulled back.

"Don't think, Gavin, just kiss me."

She didn't have to ask him twice. With lightning speed, he captured her lips, kissing her with an intensity and need he hadn't felt in a long time, if ever. Wrapping his arm around her waist, he pulled her closer and deepened the kiss, tasting every centimeter of her mouth. Desire hummed through his veins and it wouldn't take much to for him to carry her to his bedroom. He muttered a curse when the doorbell rang. "I'll be right back."

Gavin dragged a hand down his face and tried to get his breathing under control as he made his way to the door. He hoped it wasn't Micah. He snatched it open and frowned. "Eric. Khalil. What's up?" Eric Thompson was one of the other detectives at the sheriff's department who worked with Khalil.

Khalil shook his head. "Sorry, bro."

"I'd like to talk to you about the disappearance of Monique Rivers," Eric said.

Gavin went still. "Why?"

"We're questioning everyone who might have been involved with her and I need you to come down to the station."

"I'm not involved with her. Can it wait until tomorrow? I just got in from a flight and I have a dinner guest."

"No. It can't. So, let's go."

He cursed under his breath. All he saw was his family being dragged in the headlines again. And because of the same damn family. "I'll meet you at the station as soon as I drop my guest off at home." Gavin could see the questions in Eric's eyes, but he had no intention of telling him Nadia's name. The last thing he wanted to do was bring her into his mess so soon after she'd had to deal with her own.

Eric nodded, pivoted, and loped down the steps.

Khalil hung back for a moment. "I know this is fucked up, considering what just happened to me. And to you back then."

Both Khalil and Sinceer had been questioned about Monique's disappearance. "Yeah. This is complete *bullshit*. Are you going to be there?"

"Nah, man. They know we go way back—conflict of interest and shit. But if you need me, I got you."

Gavin nodded. "I know. I guess I'd better not keep *Detective Thompson* waiting," he said sarcastically. "Let me go talk to Nadia first and take her home."

Khalil nodded, clapped him on the shoulder, then loped down the steps and headed for his car.

He resisted the urge to slam the door and stalked back to the kitchen.

Nadia quickly came to her feet. "What's going on, Gavin?"

"I have to go to the sheriff's office." He debated giving her the reason—he'd never been one to open up, but she'd shared details of her drama and he owed her that much. "They want to question me about Monique Rivers' disappearance."

"The woman that went missing last month? I saw that they'd questioned two men already."

He ran an agitated hand over his head, pissed that his dinner date had been interrupted. And pissed that whatever game Monique was playing, she continued to wreak havoc in his life. "Yeah. We're going to have to reschedule dinner. Apparently, it can't wait until tomorrow."

"That's okay." She was already putting her food back into the container.

Gavin placed it in the bag, then grabbed his keys off the counter. He waited for her to put on her shoes and escorted her to his car. Eric was still parked on the street in front of his house, watching him as if he were a criminal. Ignoring him, they got in and left. Following her directions, he pulled into the driveway of a small house less than ten minutes away with the detective right behind him. He got her bag out of the car and walked her to the door. "I'm sorry."

Nadia reached up and palmed his face. "You have no need to be sorry. This is out of your control. The sooner you answer his questions, the sooner we can get back to whatever is happening between us."

"Thanks." She came up on tiptoe and kissed him. The sweetness poured into his soul, and he wrapped his arms around her, wanting to prolong what she was beginning to make him feel.

"Call me later."

"I will." He gave her hand a squeeze and waited until she went inside before going back to his car and heading to the sheriff's office.

When he arrived at the station, Eric led Gavin into an interrogation room and gestured him to a chair. As he sat, another man joined them and Eric made the introductions.

"This is Agent Timothy Stills from the South Carolina State Law Enforcement Division. Their office will be assisting us in the investigation."

Gavin nodded at the tall, slender agent and took in the man as he leaned against the wall. His arms were crossed, a scowl lining his face.

For a moment, the detective said nothing, studying Gavin as if trying to intimidate him. What the man didn't know was

Gavin didn't scare easily, not after all he'd been through. He met Eric's gaze evenly.

A slow grin stretched across Eric's lips. "Tell me about your relationship with Monique Rivers."

"I don't have a *relationship* with her."

"I understand she attended your event at the gallery the weekend she went missing."

"Yes."

"Did you talk to her?"

"Briefly."

"I understand you two had words. What was that about?"

The only person who'd heard part of the conversation was Ms. Leah and she despised her as much as Gavin. However, she would also tell the truth. "Nothing more than her trying to bring up what happened more than twenty years ago. It lasted all of two minutes, then I asked her to leave. She did."

"And you haven't talked to her since then?"

"No." Gavin made a point of staying away from her and anyone connected to her evil ass family. "Where is this going, Detective? There are far more people in this town who have a motive."

"And you don't? We all know what her family did to yours."

His heart started pounding and he clenched his fists. He should've known Eric would dredge up the past, particularly when Eric was one of the students who'd laughed at their plight. "Again, it was years ago, and as you can see, we're fine now. So there's no *motive*," he gritted out.

"So you say. But what about you personally? I'm sure you're still angry about how she humiliated you during the college fair."

Gavin leaned forward. "Why would I still be angry? I still got the scholarship. Still went to college. Studied abroad.

Opened up a new gallery that's doing well. So again, why would I be stuck on something that happened all those years ago?" Truthfully, he hated everything about the Rivers family because of what they took from his, but he'd moved on, and saw no reason to put himself under the spotlight any more than necessary. "Now, is there anything else?"

"Yes. Where were you between Friday night and Monday morning of her disappearance?"

"I stayed at the gallery until about two in the morning, then I had a flight out Saturday afternoon to San Francisco and returned on Monday."

"What time did the gallery close?"

"I hosted a fundraising event and it ended at ten."

"What were you doing between then and when you left at two a.m.?"

"Working on a painting, finishing up some inventory and ordering supplies."

"Was anyone else there with you?" Agent Stills asked, wading into the questioning.

"No."

"What kind of painting were you working on?"

Gavin's patience was wearing thin, and he didn't understand what difference the type of painting made in this line of questioning. "A multi-panel landscape." The agent stared at him expectantly, as if waiting for Gavin to elaborate, but he said nothing.

The detective asked, "Where did you go after you left the gallery?"

"Home."

"Alone?"

"Yes."

"Can anyone corroborate your whereabouts between the time you left the gallery and when you left for the airport?"

"No.

"You didn't talk to anyone at all?"

"No. I slept, got up and packed, then drove to the airport." Eric and Agent Stills asked him several more questions—the same ones phrased differently, but his answers never wavered. Gavin checked his watch.

"You have somewhere you need to be, Mr. Black?" Agent Stills asked.

"Just wondering how much longer this is going to take."

"As long as it takes for you to answer all our questions."

"I've answered them all, two or three times."

"Let's go over this again," Eric said.

He groaned inwardly. Two hours after entering the station, Gavin pushed through the doors and strode to his car. His brother had sent him a text.

Micah: *Did you see this? (link attached) Do you need to talk?*

Gavin clicked on the link: *Renowned Artist and Gallery Owner Brought in for Questioning in Relation to Vanished Mogul.*

And so it begins again, he thought grimly.

CHAPTER 4

*M*onday afternoon, Nadia sat at her desk going over everything related to the disappearance. Gavin had called, but they only spoke briefly. She could tell he was upset and didn't press him for answers. From what she read, Monique's assistant had called the authorities because she hadn't heard from her in days and Monique hadn't come into the office after the weekend following the gallery fundraiser. She read further and saw that her car, along with some blood and tattered clothing was found abandoned along a highway about an hour outside of town. The other thing she'd found was that the woman, along with her family had been the cause of many of the townspeople losing their businesses over the years. Nadia heard the murmurings around the office that Monique wasn't liked and a couple of people had outright called her a bitch. "They'll probably need to bring the entire town in for questioning with all the mess she's done," she muttered. "Good grief." How could one person, one family cause so much hurt and pain to so many people?

She leaned back in her chair and thought about her interview with Gavin, and the way his entire posture changed when she mentioned the other gallery. She really wanted to ask again, but with everything going on with him, decided it wouldn't be the best time to broach the subject.

"Are you settling in okay?"

Nadia glanced over her shoulder and found her boss standing there. In his fifties, with a receding hairline and a belly that had seen too many beers, Keith Ford had been warm and welcoming when she arrived. "Yes, thank you."

"I admired the piece you did on the art gallery. If I hadn't already assigned the Rivers' case to another reporter, I'd have you follow up with Gavin Black about him being questioned. His family was one of the wealthiest in the town until the scandal with the Rivers put them into poverty. I'm sure it's bringing up some bad memories for him."

"I'm sure it does," she answered, schooling her features to hide her shock and horror. No wonder he didn't want to talk about his family and past. Her heart broke for him, for his family because of what they endured. She couldn't even imagine how it must have been to go from having it all to nothing. *Another man with secrets.* Still, i t added more pieces to the man who fascinated her in ways she couldn't explain. Nadia sighed. After being betrayed by one man with secrets, she really should be running in the opposite direction because she didn't want to set herself up for another poten-tial heartbreak. Gavin didn't seem to be anything like Austin, but then again, she'd only known the man a short time, so could she really be sure? However, there was something about him that wouldn't let her walk away. He wasn't a big talker—she talked enough for both of them—but he listened with his whole body and every time she spoke, she felt like she had his entire attention. The only time he seemed to open up was when it came to his art. His warm, brown eyes sparkled with excitement and his expression became less guarded.

"I can have you assist Rachel if—"

"Oh, no. That's fine. I'm sure she can handle it." No way could she go anywhere near that investigation and not have it interfere with their growing attraction. That kiss had kept her awake half the night. It had been filled with such passion that she couldn't resist another one when he'd taken her home, even with the detective watching.

"Then I'll have you work on the ongoing RICO case the mayor has been implicated in for bribery and extortion. Have Daniel get you up to speed."

"Sounds good." For this place to be such a small town, they had a lot of big city drama.

As soon as Keith walked away, she went in search of Daniel, one of the senior investigative reporters.

He handed her three thick manila folders and said, "Happy reading."

"Thanks. I think."

Daniel chuckled. "Let me know if you have any questions."

"Will do." Nadia went back to her desk and started reading the case that had started a couple of years ago. *How is this man still the mayor?* As she pored over the pages, she realized one name kept popping up: Rivers. Were they somehow involved, as well? And how? She made it through only half of one of the folders before her eyes started to glaze over.

Taking a peek at her watch, it surprised her to see that she'd been reading for over two hours and it was time to call it a day. For a minute, she contemplated whether to take them home, but decided against it. She'd done that a lot in Seattle and had promised herself that she would do better separating work from home. After locking everything in her desk, she straightened up and called out goodbyes as she made her way out. Her phone chimed as soon as she got into the car. She smiled when she saw a message from her friend.

Brooklyn: *Hey, girl. Still waiting on updates about your fine artist. Did you order any of the stuff from the links I sent?*

Nadia: *No, I did not. And there aren't a lot of updates. We've both been busy. We happened to arrive at the airport the same time yesterday and he drove me home. Our dinner date got interrupted last night.* Her finger hovered over the keyboard and she debated on whether to tell her friend about the investigation. Deciding against it for the moment, she hit the send button.

Brooklyn: *Maybe you should surprise him at work. Ain't nothing like some sexy times in the office!*

Nadia: *You're crazy...lol! Only you would do something like that. Besides, he works in an art gallery. He might be painting or something.*

Brooklyn: *And I got my man. Body paint could be fun.*

Nadia: *This conversation is over.*

Brooklyn: *I'm just sayin'. Get CREATIVE!*

She burst out laughing and placed the phone in a cupholder, then started the engine.

While driving home, she decided to explore the town a little more and went in the opposite direction. On her way back, she headed down Elm Street. As she passed Reflections Fine Arts, she slowed. Without analyzing why, and telling herself it wasn't because of Brooklyn's advice, she pulled into the small lot and parked. She had no idea if Gavin would be available, but she wanted to make sure he was okay.

There were a few people inside, milling around, but she didn't see him.

"Ms. Dubois. Welcome back."

"How are you, Ms. Adams? And please call me Nadia."

"Doing well for a woman in her sixties. What brings you by today?"

"I was wondering if I could speak with Gavin for a few

minutes. Is he here?" The older woman scrutinized her for a lengthy moment, and Nadia resisted the urge to squirm under her penetrating stare. Then she smiled.

"For you, I'm sure he'll make himself available."

Ooo-kay. What does that mean? "Thanks."

"Follow me. He's in his studio working."

"Oh, that's okay. I don't want to interrupt his creative flow."

Ms. Adams waved her off. "Nonsense. Come on."

Nadia heard the music before she turned the corner. It was an orchestral violin piece infused with the unmistakable sounds of R&B—a unique combination, and she made a mental note to ask about it. The door was partially open and, instead of knocking, Ms. Adams walked right in. Nadia hung back, not wanting to intrude. Gavin sat at a long table adding pieces of clay to what looked like a woman. She stood transfixed as his hands moved rapidly, carving, trimming, his face a study in concentration.

"Gavin, there's someone here to see you," Ms. Adams said.

His head came up and he slowly came to his feet. "Nadia. Hey." Gavin wiped his hands, then covered the piece with a damp cloth. "What are you doing here?" He leaned over and turned the music down some.

"I was in the neighborhood and thought I'd stop by to see you for a few minutes. But I don't want to interrupt."

"You're fine. Did you need me to do something, Ms. Leah?"

"Nope. I'll just be out front." She divided a knowing look between Nadia and Gavin, then smiled and left.

Nadia waited a moment before speaking. "I wanted to make sure you were okay after...yesterday. I saw the headlines."

"I'm dealing with it."

She nodded. "Hopefully, it'll be over soon, and the police can find the real culprit."

"I hope so."

"Um…what are you working on? Never mind. I know artists sometimes don't want to show their work until it's finished."

A slight smile tilted the corner of his mouth. "True, but I'll make an exception for you." Gavin removed the cloth. "It's a bust of my grandmother."

She moved closer to the table. "This is incredible. The detail is so, so amazing. Did you do this from a photo?" The woman sat at a pottery wheel, her head slightly bent, a smile on her face as her hands curved around what could've been a bowl or vase.

"No. It's from my memory."

She snapped her head around. "Are you *kidding* me? How is that possible?" He probably thought she was crazy with the way she carried on, but Nadia had never seen anything so moving. He'd told her she passed away years ago, yet he could still remember her face clearly. She could see the love he'd obviously had for his grandmother in every line, every curve of the sculpture. "You must have some kind of photographic memory or something."

"I spent a lot of time with her while she sculpted, so it wasn't that difficult."

"Do you plan to sell it?"

"No. It's personal."

Nadia leaned down to get a better look. Even her fingers had been done with such detail, and she could see the slight wrinkles in her aged hands. She couldn't stop staring. "I wish I could learn to do something half as good as this. I'm just sorry she isn't here to see what a gifted artist you are. She would be so proud."

"I appreciate you saying that, and I hope so." Gavin cleared his throat. "If you want to learn, I'll teach you."

"That sounds like fun, but don't expect mine to turn out anywhere like this. I'll be lucky if I can just do a simple cup or bowl without it looking warped."

He chuckled. "It takes practice, but I'm sure you can handle it."

"If you say so," she said skeptically. Then she thought about something. "Ooh, when we're working on it, will it be like that scene from the old movie *Ghost* with Demi Moore?"

His eyes locked on hers, he said, "It can be."

Just like that, the mood went from playful to sensual. She tried to look away but couldn't. They stood staring at each other for several charged seconds before he stepped around her, closed the door and turned the lock. He closed the distance between them, lowered his head, and touched his mouth to hers, once, twice, before kissing her fully. Moaning, she slid her arms around his waist, not caring that she'd probably have clay stains on her top. She just wanted to feel every inch of him.

"You're getting your shirt dirty," he murmured against her lips, as if he'd heard her thoughts.

"I don't care."

"You will when it's ruined."

"I'll just buy another one. Stop talking and kiss me again." Laughing softly, he trailed butterfly kisses along her jaw. Nadia's head fell back and her eyes closed as his lips and tongue journeyed over her neck and down to the tops of her breasts. Her legs trembled and she braced her hands on the table to steady herself. His hands went to her blouse, and he deftly undid each button, placing kisses over each newly bared inch of skin. Nadia's heart pumped in her chest and her breathing increased. "Gavin," she whispered.

"What, baby?"

The way he called her baby in that deep, melodic voice made her weak and she gripped the table tighter. "Somebody might...*ohh*...somebody might come in."

"No one comes in when my door is closed. And since Ms. Leah has been trying to match me up with every available woman in and out of town, she's definitely not going to interrupt," Gavin said, still kissing his way across her chest.

Nadia was two seconds from asking him to make love to her and she needed to slow down. One, they'd only known each other a month, and two, contrary to his assurance that no one would come knocking at the door, she didn't want to be the next headline. Her body, however, disagreed and wanted everything this man had to give. Here and now.

He lifted his head and redid her buttons. "The first time I make love to you will be in a bed, not an art studio."

"What about the second time?" The words tumbled out before she could stop them. Slapping a hand over her mouth, she groaned. "I was so not supposed to say that out loud. I've never said anything like that to a man. You must think I'm—" *Damn that Brooklyn!*

He silenced her with another soft kiss. "I think that you're a beautiful woman who knows who she is and what she wants. If it makes you feel better, I had the same thought the first night you asked me to teach you to paint."

The man tempted her beyond reason and she needed to leave now. "I'd better go before we both get into trouble."

"I ain't afraid of a little trouble, are you?" He tossed her bold wink.

Seeing this playful side of him enticed her even more. "Yeah. Leaving." Nadia spun around and started for the door.

"You might want this."

She turned back saw her purse dangling from his fingers, a playful glint in his eyes. Snatching it, she rushed out of the room and almost ran into Ms. Adams. "I'm sorry. I didn't see you."

Once again, wise eyes studied Nadia. "No, I suspect you didn't. Is that clay on your shirt?"

Just great. "I was leaning too close to the sculpture and I guess it touched my top," she lied.

"Hmm."

"I'll see you later. Have a great evening." She moved past the woman, not giving her a chance to respond, and hustled herself out of the building. Settled in her car a minute later, she turned the car on, cranked the air up to its highest setting and leaned her head back. Nadia sat up straight, dug out her phone and sent a text to Brooklyn: *I am NEVER speaking to you again!*

Brooklyn's reply popped up almost immediately: *Aw, hell yeah! That means you took my advice and stopped by the gallery. It must've gotten a little hot! I know it was worth every single second.*

Yeah, worth *every* second. Her head fell back again. When she relocated, she'd told herself she needed a break from men, especially after the fiasco with her ex. But who knew a few weeks later she'd meet a man who stirred her emotions in a way no other man had done, even though he seemed to have a cloud of mystery surrounding him? And be bold enough to make the first move with him. *I am in so much trouble.*

CHAPTER 5

*G*avin had put off talking to his family after being questioned for almost two weeks because he didn't want to see the pain in their eyes. And because he felt guilty for being the cause of their torment, even though there wasn't one shred of evidence to connect him to Monique's disappearance. There had been a few whispers and stares, but unlike years ago, this time no one had been outright cruel. His mother had called crying hysterically after seeing the headline, and he knew she been reliving the past. Even after all these years and though the family's wealth had been pretty much restored, she still had bouts of depression and the least little thing would send her anxiety climbing through the roof. According to Micah, she'd had to be sedated for the first couple of days, but was doing much better now. So he decided it was time to pay them a visit.

Climbing the steps the house that boasted a porch similar to the original family home, he stuck his key in the lock and let himself inside. His father must have heard him and came rushing toward the front.

"Hey, son." Gavin, Sr. pulled him into a strong hug, his

strength belying his slight build and of someone approaching seventy. His father stood a few inches shorter than him, had graying temples and a few lines bracketing his dark brown face. "How're you holding up?"

He stared into a face and eyes reminiscent of his own. "Better. I'm sorry."

His father shook his head. "I don't want to hear that kind of talk. You didn't do anything. With all the mess she and those Rivers caused in this town, it could be anybody."

Gavin couldn't refute that truth. The number of family businesses that had been lost or stolen attested to it. Back then, they hadn't been the only ones dropped below the poverty line. "How's Mom?"

He hung his head. "She's coming along."

"And the two of you?"

"We're okay. Been okay for a little while now. I shouldn't have been so distant to her back then," he finished in an agonizing whisper.

The marriage had floundered for several years as a result of everything, but neither of them had ever hinted at divorce as an option. He'd noticed some positive changes over the past decade or so and was happy to hear they were completely on track now.

"Gavin, baby." His mother rushed over and wrapped her arms around him in a crushing hug. She leaned back and palmed his cheeks. "Are you okay?"

"I'm fine, Mom. I was more worried about you." He embraced her again and kissed her temple. Despite all she'd been through, with her petite stature and honey brown skin, she could've passed for someone twenty years younger than her sixty-five years.

"I'm all right now. It's just that…that…" She ran a hand over the ponytail streaked liberally with gray that hung down her back.

"I know, and it's okay. You should come check out the new pieces in the gallery," Gavin said, trying to lift her mood. Though he hadn't been able to convince her to take up painting again, she would stop by to see the artwork sometimes.

She brightened. "I'll do that. Do you want something to eat?"

"No. I'm good."

"Well, come on back and talk to us for a minute."

He followed his parents to the covered deck at the back of the house and sat in one of the cushioned chairs placed around a fire pit they used in cooler weather.

"So, why did they call you in?" his father asked.

Before he could answer, the sliding glass door opened, and his brother stepped out.

"Hey." Micah waved their parents back down. "Don't get up." He kissed their mother's cheek and hugged their father before greeting Gavin. "What's up, big brother?"

"Not much." Gavin shifted his gaze back to his father to answer the question. "Monique showed up at the fundraiser. I thought everyone was gone, went to lock the doors, and she was still there. She tried to bring up the old stuff again and I put her out. Ms. Leah came in on the tail end, so that's how Eric knew we'd had *words*, as he called them." Ms. Leah had been beside herself with worry and guilt after finding out Gavin had been questioned, and apologized over and over until he assured her that it was okay.

"Somebody should've—"

Gavin stopped his brother's words with a glare.

His mother shook her head. "I know Leah was upset. She called me, apologizing. I told her I know you didn't have anything to do with that woman disappearing." She stood. "I'm going to start dinner. You sure you don't want to stay, Gavin? Are you staying, Micah?"

"I have a few things to take care of, but I'll be here for the next one."

"You know I'm not missing a Sunday dinner with your cooking, Mom," Micah said.

A smile blossomed on her face. "Good. Honey, can you help me get some things off the top shelf?" she asked her husband.

"Of course." He pushed to his feet and trailed her inside.

"I'm glad they're doing better," Gavin said to his brother, following their departure.

"You and me, both. Between you and me, I'm glad Monique is missing and I hope she stays gone. It'll be better for everybody in town."

"Yeah."

"Has Eric said anything else?"

"Nothing other than he's going to check out my alibi. I don't know why it's taking this long, aside from him being an ass." Eric had been among the people whispering behind his back for years. It still incensed Gavin that he'd even brought up that school incident.

"If they haven't found anything in all this time, I doubt they will. Anyway, I've been meaning to ask you about that woman at the fundraiser you were talking to."

"I talked to a lot of people that night."

"But you only had eyes for one. It was hard *not* to see when both of you were staring at each other all night. So what's up with you two? And isn't she the new reporter at the Post?"

"Yes, Nadia is the new reporter. She was there to do a story on the gallery."

Micah leaned back in the chair and stroked his chin, a grin spreading across his face. "I know I'm younger than you, but I wasn't born yesterday, so stop stalling. It's about time for you to settle down with a woman. Mama wants some grandchildren."

"I don't see your ass rushing down to get married." Their mother had made it no secret that she wanted lots of grand-children, and couldn't understand why he and Micah hadn't found a nice girl. But most of the women living in the town were the same ones who had a front-row seat to the mess back then, and had treated him like shit. No way would he even think of starting any kind of relationship with them. They had been cruel, but quickly changed their tune when the money came back.

"Not yet, anyway. At least I've had a few long-term rela-tionships. Can you say the same?"

Sometimes, he hated having a younger brother. And no, he couldn't. His high school girlfriend had shown her true colors the moment the scandal came to light. He would never forget her words: *I don't want to be with someone poorer than me. I want to live the good life, and now you can't give it to me.* It ended up being in his favor, since she was on her third or fourth marriage now. If he dated, it tended to be a woman who lived in Rosewood Heights or who hadn't lived in town back then. Still, he'd kept his heart closed. Those liaisons had never lasted more than a few weeks, and they were wholly physical in nature. Nadia was the first woman who stimulated him physically and emotionally, and the hard casing over his heart had started to crack like damp clay fired in a kiln.

"I take it by your silence I'm right. I know our life was shitty for a while and a lot of the women here were straight up mean girls. It's hard to let go of that. For both of us. But I've been talking to a counselor and realize I can't allow them to steal any more of my life. *We* can't. It's time for you to be happy, Gavin, and if Nadia does that for you, go for it. She's fine as hell, by the way—thick thighs, apple-round ass—so you'd better be glad you saw her first and I respect you as my big brother. Otherwise, I'd push your old ass in the lake and go for her myself."

He shot him a dark look. "You'd have to be able to kick my *ass* first, and we both know that ain't happening."

His brother stared. "So that's how it is, huh?"

"That's exactly how it is." He jumped to his feet. "Now, I'm going home."

Chuckling, Micah followed suit. "If you're this possessive already, I hope she's the one."

Gavin said his goodbyes to his parents, then drove home. He had initially planned to go to the gallery first, but changed his mind. His cellphone rang and he engaged the Bluetooth. "Hello."

"Gavin, it's Detective Thompson."

His heart started pounding. "What can I do for you, Detective?"

"I'm calling to let you know your alibis checked out. You're clear."

"Glad to hear it. Thanks." The tone of Eric's voice let Gavin know he didn't want deliver the message, but Gavin didn't care. Now, he could get back to his life. Relief spread across his chest. A few minutes later, he turned into his driveway and got a second shock. Nadia sat on his porch swaying slowly on the swing. He got out and smiled. As he came closer, he saw her pensive expression. "Hey. Everything okay?"

Nadia stilled the swing. "I'm sorry I didn't call first, but you said I could come whenever. I needed a place to think."

"You're fine." He sat next to her, reached for her hand and used his foot to set the swing in motion again. "What's going on?"

"He called me again. I don't know why he's so anxious to

find out my source. Unless he's involved, too. That has to be the reason," she added seemingly to herself.

Gavin went still. He knew she meant her ex. "Did you report it to the police? They should be able to do something. At the very least, you might want to get a restraining order." The man had to be out of his mind to keep harassing her when she didn't even work for the paper anymore and lived elsewhere. "Does he know where you live?"

"Absolutely not. Only my family and a few good friends do, and they can't stand him, so none of them would even give him the time of day. As far as reporting it, I called the same officer from the first time and he said he would talk to Austin."

"Good." *For Austin's good health, he'd better keep his punk ass in Seattle.*

Nadia gave his hand a gentle squeeze. "How are you? Any word on the investigation?"

"Actually, Eric called me a few minutes ago to tell me I'm all clear."

"I am *so* happy. I know it's a huge relief, especially to your family. Gavin, I... Never mind."

"What?"

She shook her head. "It's nothing."

Gavin shifted and turned her face toward his. "Tell me."

She bit her bottom lip as if nervous and hesitated a beat, then said, "I heard a little about what happened with the Rivers family. I didn't go behind your back and look it up," she added hastily. "My boss mentioned it."

Standing, he walked to the edge of the porch, shoved his hands in his shorts pockets and sucked in several deep breaths. *And so it begins.* Every time a woman found out about his past, they viewed him differently. "What exactly did he say?"

"He said that I'd done a good job on the art piece and he

would've assigned me to cover the story of your questioning if he hadn't already assigned it to another reporter. For the record, I would've declined given our relationship. He also said that your family was one of the wealthiest in the town until a scandal with the Rivers."

He didn't respond or turn around, but felt her standing behind him.

Sliding her arms around his waist and resting her head on his back, she said emotionally, "I am *so* sorry your family had to go through that kind of pain, and I can't imagine how difficult it must have been, especially at school because kids can be cruel. Everything I've heard about them says they aren't good people. But look at you now. You survived. I don't know if I would've been as strong. You didn't let her or her family break you. If they had, we wouldn't have met and that would've been a shame."

Gavin's emotions surged and nearly overwhelmed him. He'd already started falling for her, but her words made him fall harder, and she'd earned the right to hear his story. Or at least some of it.

"The Rivers had always wanted to rule everything and didn't care who they hurt in the process. We had more money, and I guess they didn't want the competition, so they got the bank to call in the loan. When my father couldn't pay it, the bank sold the art gallery that had been in my mother's family for two generations. They wouldn't even give my father a small loan just so we could keep a roof over our heads and food on the table. The strain caused my grand-mother to have a stroke, stress on my parents' marriage, and my mother to fall into depression. We lost everything. No home, no food or clothes, and no medical insurance to help my grandmother. We ended up moving into my grandpar-ents' two-bedroom, one bath house. I was a senior in high school, and they'd had to use my college fund to stay afloat."

He closed his eyes as the memories came back. "But that had run out, too. My only way out was to get a scholarship. We had a college fair, and Monique thought it would be the perfect time to humiliate me. She told everyone there that the suit I had on had been a cast off of her father's. I heard the sound of her laugh and all those kids in my head for years."

Nadia's gasp pierced the silence. "Oh, my goodness, no." She tightened her arms around him. "But I don't understand why they would do something like that. Every town or city has multiple wealthy families, so why target yours?"

"I have no idea. Greed maybe, or just pure evil." They were both, in his mind.

"It just doesn't make sense."

"Evil never does. I promised myself that I would do whatever it took to make sure we never had to suffer like that again."

She came and stood in front of him. "And you did."

Gavin gently wiped away her tears. This beautiful woman was crying for him. Every moment he spent around her chipped away at the layers of pain and resistance around his heart. "I'm okay now." She came up on tiptoe and kissed him, filling it with passion, comfort, and reassurance. Gavin quickly took over the kiss, bringing her closer to the fit of his body and wanting her to feel just how hard she made him. How much he wanted her. She moaned and trembled, writhing against him and sending heat flowing through his veins. Gavin felt his control slipping. Then sanity returned. They were standing on his front porch where anyone could see them and he didn't want anyone in his personal business. "Let's go inside. I don't want to give my neighbors anything to talk about." He unlocked the door, swept her into his arms and carried her over the threshold. Kicking the door closed, he strode down the hallway to his bedroom and placed her on her feet. The kisses began again while his hands roamed over her body. Her hands were just as busy. Nadia slid them beneath his shirt, her touch making him shudder. He tore his mouth away and rested his forehead against hers, their breathing harsh and uneven. "Nadia," he whispered.

She placed a finger on his lips. "Don't talk, Gavin. Make love to me."

Those had to be the sweetest words he'd ever heard. Gavin laid her on his bed and slowly, erotically removed each layer of her clothing, licking, kissing and touching every inch of her beautiful body as if she were a priceless piece of art. He trailed his tongue between the valley of her breasts, then circled the tips, sucking in first one, then the other.

"Gavin, I *ohhh*," she said with a groan, her back arching off the mattress.

The sweet sounds of her rising passion fueled his own. Gavin charted a path down the front of her body and slid one finger inside of her. Her moans increased as he added another one and sank deeper into her wetness. He kissed her again, his tongue mimicking the movements of his fingers. Her feminine muscles clenched his fingers and she moved her hips in time with his rhythm. Using the pad of his thumb, he circled her clit.

Nadia broke off the kiss and screamed his name as she convulsed all around his fingers.

Gavin eased his fingers out, and she whimpered. "I got you, sweetheart. Don't worry. We're not done." He rose from the bed and stripped in seconds, then removed a trio of condoms from the nightstand drawer. He tore one off, sheathed himself, and climbed back onto the bed, sliding his body over hers. They both moaned. "Damn, girl. You feel so good."

"Mmm, so do you. I love touching you. Your body reminds me of one of your sculptures." She reached between them and wrapped her hand around his shaft, slowly moving up and down.

He shuddered from her words as much as her touch. The way she stroked him had him ready to explode and he clamped a hand down on hers. Resting his forehead against hers, he said, "You're killing me, baby." Gavin raised himself up and positioned his erection at her opening. Their eyes locked as he eased inside of her, going deeper and deeper. He lowered his head and sucked in a sharp breath as a myriad of emotions filled him. He started with short strokes and gradually lengthened them, but kept the pace slow, his eyes never leaving hers. She wrapped her legs around his waist and arched her body as he changed the rhythm, moving faster and faster. Gavin buried his face in her neck and released a guttural moan. "You feel so good, sweetheart. Do you feel what you're doing to me?" His body trembled and he captured her mouth again in a hungry kiss.

"Yes, because you're doing the same thing to me," she whispered against his lips. "Don't stop."

He had no intention of stopping until they were both satisfied. He lifted her hips in his hands, quickening the pace. Her nails raked down his back and palmed his flexing butt as he thrust deeper. Their groans and cries echoed throughout the bedroom and Gavin felt his orgasm rising.

"*Gavin!*"

He lifted her higher, pounded into her until her body exploded. She screamed. He kept pumping and she exploded again, screaming even louder. Her body shook uncontrollably, and she moaned loud and long.

Gavin went rigid and his body bucked as he reached his own climax. Her name tumbled from his lips on a deep moan. Their orgasm seemed to go on forever and it took several minutes for their breathing to return to normal. He shifted his weight slightly and caressed her face. Leaning down, he kissed her tenderly. She stared at him with such a caring look, it made his heart clench. A sense of peace surrounded him like nothing he had ever experienced.

"I hope she's the one." Micah's words came back to him. So did he.

～

Three days later, Gavin still couldn't stop thinking about his evening with Nadia. Or the fact that he'd shared part of his past with her, though he'd withheld the emotional turmoil he had experienced. He hadn't expected her response or the explosive passion that had flared between them. After that first round, they'd taken a short nap, show-ered, and together prepared a quick bite to eat. Halfway through the meal, Nadia had excused herself from the table for a minute, then came back and whispered in his ear just how much she enjoyed his touch, his kiss and the way he'd made love to her, what she wanted him to do to her again, and dropped a condom in front of him. He turned and there she stood naked. Before she could blink, he'd dropped his pants, rolled on the condom and had her against the wall. Even now, her scent, her whimpers and the way she called his name made his erection throb. Sucking in a deep breath, Gavin stood in the gallery showroom trying to remember what he was doing. *Paintings. Moving the paintings.*

Shaking himself, he continued rearranging the paintings to make room for an eight-painting collection due to arrive that day. As he finished rehanging the final one, the front door chimed and he smiled at the beautiful woman entering. Gavin rushed to meet her. "Michaela Saunders. It's good to see you." They embraced.

Laughing, she said, "I go by Michaela *Prescott* now." She'd married into the wealthy Prescott family that lived across the river in Rosewood Heights.

"My bad." He'd met Michaela at an art show years ago where they both had pieces. They'd been placed next to each other and struck up a conversation, which had blossomed into a decade-long friendship. "And who is this beauty?" The toddler clung to Michaela's hand, peeking from behind her.

"This is my three-year-old whirlwind, Jordyn. She tends to be shy around strangers and takes a while to warm up."

Gavin hunkered down in front her. "Hi, Jordyn. You're a beauty just like your mama." She stared at him for a few seconds before easing away from Michaela, then a full grin spread across her small face and she lifted her hands to him. He scooped her up and placed a kiss on Jordyn's cheek. She leaned over and repeated the gesture, then laid her head on his shoulder, catching Gavin completely off guard. He'd never really contemplated fatherhood because it required him to open his heart, but this sweet little girl set off a longing so strong, he had to close his eyes for a moment.

"I don't believe it," Michaela said. "Aside from Hunter, his father, and his brothers, she has never done that with a man. She must sense you have a good heart."

"Or something," Gavin said. "Where's Hunter?"

"He should be coming through the door in a second with the paintings." She glanced around the room. "This is gorgeous, Gavin, and I can't thank you enough for showing my pieces."

"I promised you I would whenever I got it up and running." Though at that time, he had no idea if he'd ever be able to make good on it. The door chimed again and Hunter Prescott entered with the paintings on a dolly.

"What's up, Gavin?" Hunter said, coming to where they stood. "It's been a while."

"A long while."

"Daddy!" Jordyn nearly leapt out of his arms to get to her father.

Michaela chuckled. "I should've warned you. She's a hardcore daddy's girl. No one exists when he's around."

Cradling Jordyn in his arms, Hunter kissed the little girl's temple and smiled. "Don't hate."

She rolled her eyes.

Hunter brushed a kiss across Michaela's lips. "Don't worry, baby. You'll always be my number one."

The love shining between them was so evident, it made Gavin feel as if he were intruding on a private moment.

"Whatever," she said, but she was smiling. "What about you Gavin? Any woman getting closer to being Mrs. Black?"

Nadia's face flashed in his mind. He admitted to himself that he'd fallen for her, but marriage hadn't entered his thoughts. Did he dare hope that she could be the one with whom he would entrust his heart?

Hunter laughed. "I recognize that look. A little piece of advice, Gavin. Don't fight it." He smiled down at Michaela. "It's worth it. Trust me. Jordyn and I will take a look around while you and Gavin handle business." He strolled away.

Gavin didn't respond, but said instead, "I'm glad things worked out with you two." He recalled the wedding being called off hours before they were to exchange vows and Hunter being gone for a good year before the two were reunited.

"Me too. It wasn't easy and I know that everyone was angry with him for the ways things went down, but he actually did have a good reason…a life or death one." She waved a hand. "We'll talk about that another time. I know you have a lot on your plate." She removed the cloths covering the paintings of various sunsets.

"These are exquisite, Michaela." They spent an hour discussing details and made plans for the upcoming show.

When they finished, Michaela stood. "Gavin, again, I appreciate you. I've heard so many good things about the gallery, even in LA. I'm looking forward to showing closer to home this time."

"How long will you be here?"

"Just through the weekend. We're going to hang out with the family for the next few days. Hunter needs to get back for a few meetings on Monday."

"If I don't see you before you leave, have a safe trip, and I'll call you to finalize everything." Gavin spoke with the couple for a few minutes longer, then saw them out.

On the heels of their departure, Knox entered and he greeted his friend with a rough hug. "What are you doing here in the middle of the day?" Knox worked as an environmental engineer.

"I saw the paper yesterday and I know you're relieved."

"Yeah, man, I am." The Post had run an article stating that Gavin had been cleared and was no longer a suspect. His family had been relieved, too.

"This had to be hard on your parents, especially Ms. Vera."

"It was like reliving the nightmare all over again, but it's over and I can finally put this shit behind me."

"I hear you. Let's head down to Sinceer's place for a quick drink to celebrate."

"I'm down. Let me talk to Ms. Leah first to let her know I'm leaving." He went to the office and told his assistant that he was stepping out for a few minutes, then returned. The two men hadn't gone more than a few steps up the street when they saw Khalil approaching with a grim expression, his gaze trained on Knox. Gavin and Knox shared a look, and Gavin knew it didn't bode well for his friend. *Damn.*

CHAPTER 6

*N*adia sat at her desk Thursday poring over the RICO case, but her mind kept straying to her time with Gavin over the weekend. It had been something straight out of her fantasies, but her imagination hadn't come close to reality. The man had made her past encounters seem like a waste of her good time, and she was eager for a repeat performance. She still couldn't believe she'd walked into his kitchen, butt-naked, whispered in his ear that she wanted him to take her hard and fast against the wall and dropped the condom on the table. The man brought out a side of her she never knew existed. She smiled. *And I like it.* Her smile faded when their conversation on the porch came back to her. Every time she thought about what the Rivers had done to Gavin's family, tears misted her eyes. Her heart broke for all he'd gone through, and although it probably wasn't nice to speak ill of the missing, a part of Nadia hoped the woman stayed gone.

Refocusing on the report in front of her, she made more notes and wondered why the town still allowed Sherman Duncan to even walk into the mayor's office. And he was the church pastor's brother. *Somebody needs to lay some praying hands on him.* She'd tried to get an appointment to talk to him twice, but kept getting the brush-off by his assistant. On her one trip to his office, she happened to catch him briefly and only found out one thing for sure—the man annoyed her to no end with his pompous attitude. She was so lost in her thoughts, it took a moment for her to hear the chime on her phone. She picked it up and smiled when she saw Gavin's name on the display.

Gavin: *If you're not busy around 1p, how about we meet at the park and have dessert?*

Nadia: *I can definitely make time for dessert, especially if it's peach cobbler. Where's the park?* Even though the town was small, she still hadn't taken much time to drive around and find all the spots, but she had gone to the bakery a couple of times and tried samples of the cobbler, apple pie and chocolate chip cookies. The peach cobbler won, hands down.

Gavin: *Not far from the gallery. We can meet here and walk over together.*

Nadia: *Works for me.*

She set the phone on her desk. That gave her a little while longer to wade deeper into the mayor's dealings. Nadia worked steadily over the next two hours. She recalled Gavin mentioning that he would be working with a few of the recent high school graduates on some pieces they wanted to add to their portfolio, and decided to go over a little early, curious about his role as instructor.

Nadia loved not having to drive miles to get to a place. Here, she could run all of her errands and not drive more than ten or fifteen minutes. She parked at the gallery, changed into the tennis shoes she kept in her car, and went inside. She heard Gavin's deep voice the moment the door opened. Instead of walking fully into the room, she stood just out of sight and observed the four young adults in front of easels, their faces a picture of concentration. Gavin seemed to be a natural as he explained concepts and went around to each one, assisting, gently correcting, and praising their work. As if sensing her presence, he turned her way and smiled. It went straight to her heart. *I'm falling in love with him.* The thought shocked her. She didn't fall in love easily or quickly, and tended to be very cautious with her heart. But with Gavin... Nadia closed her eyes and drew in a deep breath. *Please don't let this be a mistake.*

"You okay, Nadia?"

Her eyes popped open. "Gavin. Hey. Yeah, I'm fine. I was just thinking about something." She hadn't even heard him approach and glanced around him to see the students packing up. "You're great with them."

He gestured for her to follow him. "Thanks. Have you decided when you want to start your lessons?"

As the students put away their supplies, Nadia had a chance to see the partially finished landscape pieces. "Not if you're expecting mine to come out anywhere close to these. I might need to reconsider, unless you have a paint-by-number kit. That may be a better option."

Folding his arms across his sculpted chest, Gavin gave her an amused look. "I don't know about you, woman."

She shrugged. "I'm just sayin'. No need to embarrass myself." One of the students called out to Gavin and he excused himself. She viewed the exchange with a smile. The student's animated expression to whatever Gavin was saying let her know he would be a great father. *Where the hell did that thought come from?* First, the whole falling in love thing, and now children. *Get a grip, Nadia Jonelle Dubois. You're getting way ahead of yourself.* Usually, she disagreed with that annoying inner voice, but today they were in total agreement.

"Ready?" Gavin said to Nadia after seeing the last student out.

"Yep." Entwining their hands as if it were the most natural thing, the two of them strolled around the corner to the bakery to pick up dessert. Afterwards, they crossed the street and headed the two blocks to the park. Falls Recreational Park turned out to be a beautiful place with majestic trees, walking paths, a playground, several benches, and two large gazebos that would be perfect for a family picnic. "I didn't realize this was here. It's a lovely place. Peaceful."

"It is. And now that school is back in, it's quieter during the day. We can sit here." He pointed to a bench up ahead sheltered beneath a huge tree. Ever the gentleman, he waited until she sat before lowering himself next to her.

Nadia handed him one of the small containers of peach cobbler and a spoon, then opened her own and spooned up a portion. An involuntary moan slipped from her lips as she savored the sweet treat. "I could eat this every day. Of course, my butt and thighs won't think it's a good idea."

Gavin slanted her a glance. "For the record, I really like your butt and thighs. There's not one thing wrong with them."

"There will be if I indulge like this on a regular basis," she said, pointing her spoon his way for emphasis. "I need to find a gym or something. Speaking of working out, how do you keep in such good shape?" His slim, defined muscular build didn't have an ounce of fat anywhere, despite the fact that he'd hit the forty mark.

"Working out has been a habit since my teens when I played football, so I have a gym set up at the house. Because I tend to have erratic hours at the gallery and—"

"And get lost in your art," she cut in.

"And get lost in my art, it's easier to get a workout in whatever time I feel like it."

"Well, for the record," she said, throwing his words back to him, "I really like your...everything."

Chuckling, Gavin asked, "Do you always say what's on your mind?"

"When it comes to work, yes. In my personal life, no. This is a first, and I don't know why I seem to be so comfortable doing it with you." She had never, *ever* been bold when it came to sex. That was more Brooklyn's thing. But there was something about Gavin that made her feel like...hell, she had no idea.

"I'm glad you feel at ease with me. I can say the same about you."

They shared a smile and lapsed into companionable silence as they ate. A slight breeze blew, rustling the leaves above her head. With summer winding down, the scorching temperatures had come down some, leaving the days bearable. "How is your family doing now that the whole ordeal with the missing woman is over?"

"They're good, relieved, especially my mom. I was more worried about them than me."

Reason number seventy-five why I've fallen in love with this man.

"I want you to meet my family."

Nadia choked on a piece of cobbler. Coughing, she pounded on her chest, trying to clear her throat. Her eyes watered and she gulped in air. *Meet his family?*

"Are you okay?" Gavin opened the bottle of water he'd bought and handed it to her. "Here, drink a little." He kept his concerned gaze trained on her.

She took a couple of tentative swallows. "I'm fine. Just went down the wrong way."

"More like you were caught off guard by what I said."

"Yeah. That, too." Feeling better in control, she drank a couple of sips and handed the bottle back. Since he seemed to be okay with her speaking her mind, she said, "Meeting your family is a whole other level. Are we there yet?"

"I think that's where we're headed. Don't you?"

Okay, sure she loved him, but he'd never said anything remotely close to the 'L' word. Actually, neither of them had. "I hadn't really thought about it. We're just...just dating or whatever."

He shifted on the bench to face her. "Nadia, I'm not some twenty-something kid hopping from woman to woman. I'm a forty-year-old man who found a woman that I'd like to build a relationship with. This is not a game to me. If we're not on the same page, that's cool. But if we do this, we go all the way. Am I the only one who feels what's happening between us?"

His hand covered hers and she felt the same warmth that had been there the first night they met. He spoke with such conviction and seriousness, she couldn't utter a word. A moment of panic seized her, telling Nadia it was too fast. But her heart said otherwise. Finally, she pushed the words past her lips. "No, you aren't. I feel it, too. But part of me is afraid of those feelings."

"You're not there alone, sweetheart. But as long as we're both going in the same direction, we'll be okay."

She nodded. Gavin leaned over and captured her mouth in a soft, sweet kiss filled with a tenderness that brought tears to her eyes. She needed it to stay okay.

Sunday, Gavin helped Nadia out of the car and led her up the walkway to his parent's front door. He figured Sunday dinner would be the perfect time to introduce her to his family. His brother had confirmed he'd be there too, so he could do it all in one shot. She was the first woman he'd brought home since high school and he knew they'd love her as much as he did. He still couldn't believe he'd fallen in love with her within two months. Somehow, she'd shattered the wall of protection that had surrounded his heart for more than two decades just by being her beautiful, spirited self.

"Do I look okay?" Nadia smoothed a hand over the sleeveless sundress she wore.

"You look beautiful, baby. Relax." He pressed a kiss to her temple. "My family is going to love you."

"I can't even remember the last time a guy took me to meet his family. I'm nervous."

"If it makes you feel better, you're the first woman I've brought to meet them since prom. They're going to be surprised." Gavin knew they'd heard rumors of him being seen with a woman—living in a small town guaranteed it— but he also knew they'd assume she was just like the others. They, better than anyone, understood his need to protect his heart. In some ways, they had all shied away from developing close relationships.

Her mouth fell open. "Wait. *Whaaat?* They don't know you're bringing me?" She groaned. "Gavin," she whined.

Unlocking the door, he held it open for her to go in first. "What? It'll be fine."

She skewered him with a look. "I am *so* gonna hurt you, Gavin Black," she gritted out. "You don't just spring this kind of thing on your family. What if they don't like—" She cut herself off mid-sentence when his mother appeared in the foyer.

He laughed inwardly at both of their stunned expressions. "Hey, Mom." Gavin leaned down and kissed her smooth, brown cheek. "Mom, I want you to meet Nadia Dubois." He couldn't ever recall a time when his mother was left speechless until today.

Then a warm smile curved her lips. "Is this the young lady I've heard about from everybody but you?"

"Ah, yes."

She glared and popped him on the arm. "You should be ashamed of yourself, Gavin." Then she took Nadia's hands. "I'm so happy to meet you. Please come in so we can get to know you."

"It's really nice to meet you, too, Mrs. Black."

Leaving Gavin standing in the foyer, his mother hooked her arm in Nadia's and escorted her through the house. As soon as they made to the family room at the back of the house, he met the surprised gazes of his father and brother. Both men got to their feet.

Not giving him an opportunity to make introductions, his mother said, "This is Gavin's girl, Nadia Dubois. Isn't she a doll?"

Another round of greetings ensued, and his brother shot him a look that said they would talk later.

After everyone was seated, his father said, "Tell us a little about you, Nadia."

"I grew up in Seattle, but moved here a couple of months ago to take a job at the Post."

"Oh yeah, you're the one who did the article on the gallery," Micah said. "It was a good piece."

"Thank you. Just like I told Gavin, I take my job serious and am not in the business of sensationalizing headlines. I stick to the truth, and I believe that some things should remain confidential."

The brief look she gave him communicated that she'd wanted to assure his family that she wouldn't take advantage of them just for a headline. The gesture moved Gavin and made him love her more. Within minutes, she had him and his family laughing with a relaxed camaraderie he hadn't experienced in a long time. He enjoyed watching his mother's animated features, reminding him of how she used to be when he was a kid.

"Oh, I'm just going on and on." His mother jumped up with a jolt of energy that made Gavin smile. "Let me get this dinner finished so we can eat."

Nadia stood. "I'll help you. Whatever you're cooking smells so good and has my mouth watering."

She giggled. "It's nothing. I just threw a little something together." The two women headed to the kitchen laughing and talking.

"She seems like a nice girl, Gavin," his father said. "How did you meet a reporter, of all things?"

"She is, and she came to the fundraiser. Nadia's not like the others, Dad."

He nodded. "As long as she makes you happy."

"Honey, can you come here for a minute?" his mother called from the kitchen.

"Be right there." He eased up from his favorite recliner and left the room.

"Well, well. I never thought I'd live to see the day when my big brother fell in love," Micah said as soon as their father was out of earshot. "And you have fallen, G. *Hard.*"

Gavin couldn't deny one word. "I can't explain it. She's just...I don't know."

"You don't need to. I get it. I'm happy for you, bro." He leaned forward and grinned. "I know you, Sinceer, Khalil, and Knox are friends, but I get first dibs on being best man at your wedding."

He held up a hand. "Slow your roll, boy. Nobody said anything about marriage," he said softly.

"You didn't have to. Your face says it all when you look at her." He started humming the "Wedding March" and sat back with a smug smile.

"Shut the hell up."

Micah only laughed. "Let me know when you're ready to go shopping for tuxes."

"I will kick your ass."

He was spared from more of his brother's wisdom when his mother called them to the table. Gavin stopped short when he saw the number of dishes set out on the table. *So much for just throwing a little something together.* His mother had prepared fried pork chops, green beans, mashed potatoes, macaroni and cheese and some of her light-as-air rolls.

His father blessed the food after everyone took their seats around the table that sat six.

"Everything looks good, Mom."

"It does, and I'm going to seriously hurt myself," Nadia said, causing everyone to laugh.

Murmurs of agreement flowed around the table as they all filled their plates. For the first few moments, the only sounds heard were the scraping of forks against plates and groans of satisfaction.

"Oh, my goodness. Mrs. Black, these rolls are to die for," Nadia said. "I'd love to know where you got them."

"I got them right here."

"You made these from *scratch?*"

"I sure did," his mother said, beaming. "The recipe has been in my family for generations, and I've been waiting to pass it down to someone special." She gave Gavin a look that needed no interpretation.

Micah, hunched over his plate, laughed and said, "I'm free on Tuesday late afternoon."

Sweat popped out on Gavin's forehead and he didn't dare look at Nadia. Yes, he was glad his family liked her, but why were they all trying to rush him down the aisle?

CHAPTER 7

A week later, Nadia sat at her desk picking through the salad she'd brought for lunch. What she wouldn't give to have more of Mrs. Black's homemade rolls. When she and Gavin were leaving, the woman had packed enough leftovers to last for two days despite Nadia's protests. She'd really enjoyed her time getting to know them. While Mr. Black's quiet spirit reminded her of Gavin, Micah turned out to be the lighthearted one in the family and had kept her laughing the entire visit. With what she'd learned about them over the spectacular meal and from a few other people, she didn't understand how the Rivers could be so cruel to such a giving group of people.

It still nagged her that they'd gone after the Blacks with such tenacity. Why? The reporter in her wanted answers. There had to be some other reason, aside from the ones Gavin mentioned and she planned to do a little digging. Closing the container, Nadia stood and went to Rachel's office.

"Hey, Nadia," Rachel said, turning from her computer and removing her glasses.

"Hey. Do you have a minute?"

"Sure. Have a seat. Everything okay?" she asked with concern. The forty-something woman removed the elastic band from her hair, smoothed the stray strands back, and redid the ponytail.

"Oh, yes. Fine." Nadia sat and took a hasty peek over her shoulder to ensure no one was in hearing range. "I wanted to ask you a couple of questions about what happened with the Rivers and Blacks. You grew up here, right?"

Rachel leaned back in her chair and blew out a long breath. "I did, and it was one of the most heartbreaking things I've ever seen. I'm a few years older than Gavin, so I'd already finished college when everything went down. But I heard about how Monique humiliated him. The bitch."

She lifted a brow. "I guess there's no love lost between you two."

"No. She walked around like she was better than every-body else, and if you look in the dictionary under mean girl, you'll see her picture."

"She was that bad?"

"*Worse.*"

"But why target them that way?"

"I don't know. A lot of people wondered the same thing. The Blacks always donated to causes and helped whoever had a need."

"That was my impression when I met them, and from the little I read regarding the other art gallery they owned."

"They always had the best art shows, and Mrs. Flemming, Gavin's grandmother, used to offer a few lessons to budding artists." Rachel snapped her fingers. "You know I remember my grandmother mentioning something about some painting Mrs. Flemming had done that they wanted. She said Mr. Rivers was livid when she wouldn't sell it to him. Appar-ently, it was a personal piece, but according to my grandmother that didn't stop him from badgering her about it. From what I understand, they actually stole it, but it's been rumored that the Blacks got it back somehow. Only they claim they don't have it. Shortly after is when all hell broke loose. All the mess caused her to have a massive stroke and she died a year or so later."

"Over a painting? That doesn't make sense," Nadia said, more to herself. What could be in a painting to cause so much hatred?

"I agree, but since she's not here to explain…" Rachel shrugged.

"Do you know if Mrs. Flemming had any good friends that are still around?"

"She and my grandmother were friends, but Grandma has some dementia now and I honestly don't think she'd be able to tell you anything. There is one other woman, Olivia Roberts. Everyone calls her Ms. Olivia, but most people stay away from her because they say she's crazy."

She sat up straight, her curiosity piqued. "Why?"

"Mostly because of her rants regarding the lake being poisoned and people dying in it, and that there's evil in the town." Rachel smiled. "I recognize that look. I used to have the same one when I was intrigued by a story." She picked up a notepad and pen, wrote something on it, tore off the page and handed it to Nadia. "Ms. Olivia's address. I figured that would be your next question."

Accepting the slip of paper, she chuckled. "And that's why you're the editorial supervisor. Thanks. If I find out anything, I'll let you know."

"Please do."

"See you later." Nadia returned to her desk, got her purse and phone, then let her boss know she was stepping out to do some research. She programmed the address into her GPS and followed the directions to a house in an older section of the town that looked to have been built at least a hundred years ago. Nadia imagined it probably stood proud as a showpiece in its prime. Now, with its faded gray paint, weathered columns and porches, and overgrown yard, it just looked tired and…old.

Getting out of her car, she navigated through the brush and climbed the steps to the porch that creaked with every step. She rang the bell and studied her surroundings while waiting. Nadia whirled around when she heard the heavy door open. A tall woman with snow white hair that contrasted with her coffee-colored skin stood glaring.

"Are you lost or something?"

"Um…no, ma'am. I'm looking for Ms. Olivia."

"Who are you?" the woman asked gruffly.

"My name is Nadia Dubois and I work for The Post. I wanted to ask you a few questions, if that's okay." Ms. Olivia didn't say anything. Despite the lines bracketing her face, the eyes that bore into Nadia's were as sharp as an eagle. An involuntary shiver passed through Nadia with the frank appraisal, but she held the woman's gaze without flinching.

"You must be new around here because nobody comes to talk to me. And you don't seem to be afraid of me. Hmph. Finally, a woman with a backbone." Ms. Olivia unlocked the screen. "Come on in."

"Thank you." She followed the older woman's slow gait to a formal living room and accepted the offered seat on a floral-patterned sofa.

"Wasn't expecting visitors, so I ain't got nothing to offer you."

Stifling a smile, she said, "That's just fine. I don't want you to go through any trouble on my account. I'll try not to take up too much of your time."

Surprise registered on her face as she dropped down heavily in a recliner. "Well, what do you want to know?" She shook her head and wagged a finger at Nadia. "Now, I'm not no gossiper, so if that's why you're here, you can walk right on at that door."

"No, ma'am. I'm not here for gossip. I would like to ask you about your friend, Mrs. Flemming, and some paintings she did."

Ms. Octavia stiffened. "You mean the paintings those damn Rivers stole?"

"Yes. I recently met the Black family and they're such nice people and I can't understand why the Rivers went after the paintings and them." *And I love their son and want him to have closure.*

"Because they're just evil, plain and simple. If somebody had something, they wanted it and would do anything to get it, no matter who they hurt." She shook her head and her voice cracked. "I lost my best friend because of them, and I will hate them until the day I die." She swiped at the tears in her eyes.

"My apologies for bringing up bad memories."

"I'm fine. Go on with your questioning."

"Yes, ma'am."

"Respectful. I like that. I got some lemonade in the fridge. You want some?"

Nadia smiled at the change. "Yes, please. That would be nice."

"These old bones give me fits," she said as she eased up from the chair. "But I'm glad to still be among the living. Be right back."

While Ms. Olivia was gone, Nadia took a moment to survey the room. While all the furniture looked to be at least thirty or forty years old, it had been maintained well. Everything sat neatly in its place and there wasn't a speck of dust anywhere. A few black and white photos were lined on the fireplace mantle, and she wandered over to check them out.

She leaned closer to see one showing side views of two smiling young women posed in sleeveless A-line dresses and sandals, each with a hand on a hip. One resembled a younger Ms. Octavia, but the other one also seemed familiar. She lifted it for a closer look. Her heart started pounding. *Is that Gavin's grandmother?*

"That's me and Savannah."

Ms. Octavia's voice startled her. "Savannah Flemming?"

"Yes." A small smile curved her lips. "We were something else back then. Gave the boys fits." She handed Nadia a glass.

"I bet. Look at those hips and legs for days. Those guys probably didn't stand a chance."

For the first time, a full smile spread across her face and she chuckled. "Honey, no they didn't."

Taking a sip of the cool liquid, she placed the photo back in its place and reclaimed her seat. "This lemonade is delicious."

"Thank you." She set her own glass on the side table next to her chair before sitting. "What do you plan to do with the information I give you? I don't want to see that family suffer one more minute behind this mess and have their names dragged through the mud behind some headline you're chasing."

"Ms. Octavia, I assure you, I'm not after any headline." Nadia decided to put all her cards on the table. She wanted the woman to trust her. "I care for Gavin a lot, this is personal. None of what we discuss will be shared with the newspaper. The only people that will hear it is the Black family."

After leveling Nadia with another one of her hawk-like stares, she said, "Savannah was a gifted artist and she knew those folks were into all kinds of illegal things. She tried going to the authorities back then, but they were all in

Humphrey's back pocket, so they ignored her. So she did a trio of paintings that gave hints of what was going on."

She froze with her glass half to her mouth. "How did he know about the paintings?"

"He saw them in the old gallery one day while I was there and made an offer for them. I'm sure he took one look at them and realized what they represented. She told him they weren't for sale. He must've cursed her something awful before storming out and promising to get those paintings. Savannah wanted whoever came behind her to be able to dig into the past and stop them from doing more harm to the town. Here."

Nadia rose and took what she realized was another photo, this one in color. "The painting," she whispered. It was of the lake, with one half a deep, beautiful blue and the other half black. She peered closely and saw what seemed to be someone or something being poured onto the side that had been blackened." She handed it back.

"You can keep it."

"I was told the Rivers' stole them, but the family was able to retrieve them." She wondered about the truth of that statement because Gavin had never mentioned them, and she didn't see them at the gallery or among the many paintings that hung in his parent's house.

"That's true."

"Do you know what happened to them?"

Ms. Octavia stood abruptly, all traces of her warm demeanor now gone. "I'm tired now."

Nadia's heart rate kicked up. *She knows something.* She toyed with pressing the older woman, but decided against it, remembering the old adage her own grandmother used to say about getting more bees with honey. "I'm sorry. I didn't mean to take up so much of your time. If you'll show me where I can wash my glass, I'll get out of your hair so you can rest."

She stared at Nadia curiously for a few seconds. "You can leave it right there and I'll take care of it later."

Nodding, she got a business card from her purse and wrote her cell number on the back. "If you think of anything else, call me at the number on the back. It's my personal number and not connected in any way to the newspaper." She placed it on the table next to the chair Ms. Octavia vacated. "You don't have to walk me out. Take care of yourself, and if you need *anything*, let me know. Have a good day, Ms. Octavia."

Nadia left the woman standing there and headed back to her car. Once inside, she started the engine, stared at the photo in her hand, and debated whether to go back to the office or directly to the gallery. She chose the latter.

Ten minutes later, she was striding through the gallery doors. Gavin stood across the room talking to Ms. Leah, but excused himself when he saw her.

Gavin kissed her. "Hey, baby. What are you doing here?"

"I need to talk to you about something."

Angling his head, he frowned. "Is everything okay?"

She scrubbed a hand across her forehead. "I'm not sure."

"We can talk in my office. Come on back."

His hand in the small of her back provided some comfort from the turmoil swirling in her belly. She had no idea how he would react, but she didn't feel right keeping the information from him.

He led her to his office and closed the door. Rubbing his hands up and down her arms, he said, "Talk to me, sweetheart. I can feel the tension bouncing off you."

She hesitated, then handed him the photo. "Do you recognize this?"

His eyes widened, then a heavy scowl lined his face. "Where did you get this?"

Nadia jumped hearing the anger in his voice. "From Ms. Octavia. She said it's the painting Mr. Rivers wanted. I couldn't understand why they came after your family and started digging around."

His face went blank. "So, this is for some story," he tossed out.

"*Of course not!* This is for your family. For *you.*"

"You expect me to believe that? You go digging around in my past and what, I'm supposed to be happy about it?"

She took a deep breath, wondering if she should've just left well enough alone. "Gavin, listen to me. I promise you this will not *ever* be disclosed to anyone at the newspaper. You said you didn't understand why, and after meeting your family and seeing how wonderful they are, I wanted to find out so you all could find closure or, at the very least, have something to fight with if they tried the same tactics again." She reached for him and he shrugged her hand off. Tears filled her eyes and she felt as if he'd stabbed her in her heart.

Gavin paced the confines of the office, then stopped. "So, was this your plan all the time? Get close to me, my family, and then what?"

Anger vibrated through her. "Wait a damn minute. Exactly what are you accusing me of doing?"

He dragged a hand down his face. "Look, Nadia."

She went into full angry Black woman mode, complete with finger-pointing and neck-rolling. "No, *you* look. I would *never* do anything to hurt your family. I *told* you the day I interviewed you that I. Don't. Roll. Like. That." She jabbed her finger in his chest with each word, her voice steadily rising. "You want to know why? One, I care about you. Two, I met your wonderful family, and they didn't deserve what happened to them. I can't believe you'd think I'd be foolish enough to betray you like that." She cursed as a tear trailed down her cheek. She hated crying.

"Nadia, I'm—"

"You made me care about you. You made me lo—" She cut herself off. "I have to get out of here." Nadia spun around, snatched the door open, and ran into a solid wall.

"Nadia. Hey, girl," Micah said. "Are you okay?"

She shook her head and stormed past him. She had to leave before she completely broke down. Her chest heaved and she struggled to draw in a normal breath. Gavin's mistrust hurt far more than her ex's betrayal. Tears blurred her eyes as she nearly ran to her car. She got in, gunned the engine, and sped off. She should've listened to her first mind and walked away after the interview. Her house was only ten minutes away, but she had to pull over twice because she was crying so hard, she couldn't see. Her phone rang. She saw Gavin's name on the display and sent it straight to voicemail. A minute later, it rang again. "Stop calling me, dammit!" she yelled in the car. But it wasn't him. It was Brooklyn. Not ready to talk to her, either, she let it go to voicemail. The phone chimed with a text message soon after, and then with another one a couple of minutes later, but she ignored them both. She pulled into her driveway, hopped out and rushed up the porch.

As soon as she unlocked the door, a pair of hands grabbed her. Nadia screamed and swung her purse, catching the man on the side of his face.

"*Ow!* Shit!"

Shocked, she blinked twice. "*Austin?* What the hell are you doing here?" she asked angrily.

Eyes filled with pure hatred stared back at her. "You're going to give up that source and I'm not leaving until you do." A feral grin tilted the corner of his mouth. "We can do it the easy way, or the hard way. Your choice. Now *move!*"

"What the hell is going on, Gavin? What did you do to her?" Micah asked, glaring at Gavin.

"I screwed up. I've got to go after her." He owed her an apology and probably more after the way he'd behaved. When she'd flashed that picture and used the phrase "digging around," all his common sense went straight out the window. His heart pounded in his chest and dread uncoiled in his belly.

"Yeah, you do. And I'm driving. You look like a wreck."

Gavin didn't argue. They raced out of the gallery. "I'll be back, Ms. Leah."

"Begging might work," she said sagely.

Any other time, he might've laughed, but not today. Begging was probably...no, *definitely* at the top of his list. They jumped into Micah's SUV, and he gave him her address. Because they'd grown up there, they knew every back road. She only had a couple of minutes head start, so they should get there at the same time, or right behind her.

"What happened?" His brother maneuvered through the streets like he was on a NASCAR track.

"She had a photo of Grandma's painting."

"The one we've been looking for?" he asked with surprise.

"Yeah. She said she'd gotten it from Ms. Octavia and that she'd been digging around."

"And your ass went off the deep end."

"Something like that," he mumbled.

"G, that woman loves you, and I truly believe she wouldn't do anything to hurt you like putting our business on another headline. That's what went through your mind, wasn't it?"

Gavin slammed his hand against the dashboard. "*Shit!* Why didn't I just listen to her?" His brother was right. Nadia wouldn't do what he insinuated. The article she'd done proved it. He'd messed up big time and prayed he could fix it. The few minutes in the car on the way to her house tested his sanity.

Micah turned on her street. "Who the hell is that grabbing on her?"

"I don't know, but I'm about to find out." The car had barely come to a stop before Gavin jumped out and sprinted up the walkway to the porch where a man was trying to force Nadia into the house. He grabbed the man by the back of his shirt and yanked him back. "What the *fuck* do you think you're doing?" he roared, slamming his fist into the man's face. Ramming him against the house, he said, "Don't you *ever* put your hands on her!" He let him go, and the man slid down the wall moaning. He pulled Nadia into his arms. "Are you okay, baby?" Gavin ran his hands over her and examined her critically for any bruises or marks. If he saw one thing, the man was going to need the undertaker. Her body shook and tears stained her face. She held on to Gavin as if she never wanted to let him go. He understood. *I'm never letting her go.* "Talk to me, Nadia. Who is he?"

"My…my ex."

"Please tell me he came all the way across the country to harass you. I'm gonna whip his punk ass."

He let her go, and Micah stepped between him and the semi-conscious man lying on the porch. "Call Khalil and take care of your woman. I'll watch this fool until he gets here."

Breathing hard, his rage still running high, he dug out his phone and made the call. As he led Nadia inside, it took every ounce of his control not to stomp her ex.

"What are you doing here, Gavin?"

She might have been frightened, but not enough to forget that he'd hurt her. "Because I was wrong. And I'm sorrier than you'll ever know."

"Thanks for the apology. I think I need to be alone."

The rage turned into stark fear. He could *not* lose her. When she sidestepped his touch, the fear ramped up to panic. "Nadia, please wait."

"Why? This is too hard, and I don't want to want to have to worry about wading through the landmines of your secrets, wondering when I'll set one off."

"Please let me explain." Gavin had never been good sharing his feelings, and he'd all but shut down after his life was ruined. But for her he had to try, and maybe it was time to unburden himself.

She folded her arms but said nothing.

"Baby, I am so sorry I lashed out at you. I thought I'd moved past all the pain, the mistrust, but all it took was that one photo, to let me know that I haven't. Maybe it's time I share all the secrets that haunt me. Remember when you said that I hadn't let them break me? For a while, I *was* broken inside. And at one point, it got so bad that I stopped talking. I walked around in a daze, barely getting through the days. During those years, I had to deal with the taunting, whispering behind my back and in my face, and all I saw was the same thing happening again. In trying to protect my heart, I hurt yours. Not an excuse, just context." He slowly closed the distance between them, and when she didn't back away, it gave him a small measure of hope. "But that's on me, and I promise to do better. If you give me another chance to get it right," he added.

"I don't know, Gavin. You don't trust me, and without that, we'll never get it right. Maybe we should just cut our losses before either one of us gets hurt even more."

He took her hands in his. "That's where you're wrong, sweetheart. I do trust you. I trust you with my life, and more than that, I trust you with my heart. I know you would never do any of the things I implied. I knew it when my stupid ass words left my mouth. I heard you the day you interviewed me. I heard you in the car on the way back from the airport. I heard you here." He pointed to his heart. "I can't promise I won't ever stick my foot in my mouth again, but I know you'll call me out, and I don't have any problems with that."

"You got that right."

"Does that mean you're going to give me another chance?"

"Maybe. But only because your mom said she wanted to pass down the roll recipe to someone special and I don't want some other woman to have it," Nadia grumbled.

Gavin laughed, the weight pressing down on his chest easing. "I'll make sure you get it, and anything else you want, baby, as long as you say you'll be mine."

She eyed him. "I guess, but only because you beg pretty well."

"I'll go with that." He caressed her cheek. "I love you, Nadia."

"That's the other reason I'm giving you a chance. I love you, too."

He lifted her into his arms and his mouth came down on hers, infusing the kiss with all the love he felt in his heart.

CHAPTER 8

*G*avin parked in front of the rundown one-story home and sat for a moment. "I didn't realize it had gotten this bad."

Nadia covered his hand with hers. "I thought the same thing, and had planned to ask you if you knew someone in the area who could give it a facelift, but—."

"But that was the day I lost my damn mind." He'd been battling with the guilt since that day.

"We're past that now, Gavin. Let it go, baby. I'm not going anywhere."

He leaned over and kissed her softly. Every day for the past two weeks he'd sent up prayers of thanksgiving that she'd forgiven him, and that he had a second chance to have this amazing woman by his side. He'd also been sharing more about his past and pain, and realized that her love was slowly helping him to heal. "We should probably get out before Ms. Octavia calls the sheriff."

"Probably. People think she's crazy, but I only saw a lonely old woman who'd been robbed of her best friend. I'm going to try to visit her every now and again. If she lets me," Nadia added with a smile.

Gavin got out, came around to the passenger side and helped Nadia. Still holding her hand, they navigated through the overgrown yard to the rickety porch. "I'll get this yard done, too." He rang the doorbell.

A few moments later, the door swung open. "You look just like your daddy," Ms. Octavia said by way of greeting. She unlocked the screen and waved them in.

"How are you, Ms. Octavia?" Nadia asked.

"Same as last time you were here."

Gavin and Nadia shared a smile, and he shook his head. Ms. Octavia was still as feisty as he remembered.

"Sit and ask your questions."

He took a seat on the sofa next to Nadia, while the older woman sat across from them on a recliner that had seen its best years. "I appreciate you taking time to talk to me, Ms. Octavia. Do you know what happened to the painting from the picture you gave Nadia?"

"Yes."

He waited for her to elaborate, but she said nothing. "Would you be comfortable sharing the information with me? I know my family would be grateful for anything you can tell us."

Ms. Octavia drilled Nadia with a stare. "Young lady, this ain't gonna be in that newspaper, is it?"

"No, ma'am. Just like I told you before, this is personal and whatever you say will stay with Gavin's family." She grasped Gavin's hand and stared up at him. "I love Gavin and I only want him and his family to have some peace."

He gave her hand a gentle squeeze.

"Hmph. About time one of you boys found somebody." She pushed up from the chair and walked out.

"Oo-kay. Does that mean we're dismissed?" Nadia asked.

"Are you coming or not?" Ms. Octavia yelled out.

"I guess not," Gavin said with a laugh. "She is a trip."

"Amen."

They found her in the hallway and followed her to a closed door at the back of the house. She unlocked the door and stepped back.

"I can't go down those steps on account of my hip. You'll find the paintings on the right side wrapped in paper."

"There's more than one?"

"Three. Light switch is on the wall to your left."

Gavin's heart pounded in equal parts excitement and nervousness. *We're finally going to have a piece of our history back.* He flipped the switch, and the bulb fluttered a few times before giving off a dim light. He carefully navigated down the steep steps, batting away spider webs along the way. A thick layer of dust covered every inch of the room.

"Don't touch nothing else."

"I won't." On the far side of the cluttered space, he spotted the three large wrapped rectangles. Peeling back the corner of one, he sucked in a sharp breath. He'd recognize his grandmother's work anywhere. Gavin gathered the canvases and headed back upstairs. "Ms. Octavia, I don't know how to thank you," he said emotionally.

"Thank Giselle. That sweet girl didn't deserve what those horrible people did." She pointed a finger. "I know they did something to her. She wouldn't have just left her family."

"Giselle?"

She nodded. "Showed up one night and asked me to take care of them until she came back for them. With Savannah being gone, and you all already dealing with that damn Humphrey and his bitch of a wife, Cora," she said bitterly, "Giselle thought it best to keep them elsewhere. I don't know what you plan to do with them, but you'd better hope you don't wake up none of that evil that stole my best friend and your cousin."

Gavin had wondered the same thing and wished there was some way to find out the truth. *Is she buried somewhere in town, or had someone dumped her body elsewhere?* But her last statement gave him pause. *Wake up evil?* What kind of evil? A hand on his arm drew him out of his thoughts.

Nadia slid her arm around his midsection. "Are you okay?"

"Yeah, fine. Just a lot to digest. Ms. Octavia, no one will ever know that you had these paintings. I promise."

"I know Savannah's happy to know they're back where they belong."

He set the trio of paintings against the wall and engulfed Ms. Octavia in a strong hug. "Thank you," he whispered, a heartbeat from breaking down.

Ms. Octavia patted his back a couple of times and stepped out of his embrace. "No need for all that. I'm only doing what I promised I would do." Her gruff words were a direct contrast to the tears shining in her eyes. "Y'all go on now, and let an old woman get back to her day." She locked the basement door and led them to the front door.

"I'll come over on the weekend to do your yard, and I'll send Micah to assess what needs to be done on the house, and he'll take care of it." His brother was part owner of the town's construction company.

"I don't need no handouts."

"Grandma would want us to look out for her friend, and that's what we're going to do. If you think of anything else that you need, I want you to call."

"And you have my number," Nadia said.

Ms. Octavia's gaze softened. "Well, okay."

Smiling inwardly at winning that small battle, he and Nadia left. Gavin headed directly to the gallery.

"When are you going to tell your family?" Nadia asked after he locked them in the vault.

"I'll probably call them tonight or tomorrow and have them come by to take a look. I can't believe we have them back." Taking Ms. Octavia's words to heart, he thought it best they remained locked away for the foreseeable future. He framed her face with his hands and placed butterfly kisses on her forehead, eyelids, and cheeks. "Thank you for this. I don't know how I'll ever repay you for such a precious gift."

"Love me, Gavin. That's all I need."

"And *you're* all I need. I love you, sweetheart. So much."

"I know this has been an emotional day for you and I have just the thing to take your mind off all this."

"What?" he asked, still trailing kisses along her jaw and the exposed column of her neck.

"You told me creating art helps you. Today's the perfect time for my first lesson."

His head came up. "You're finally ready for your art lessons?"

"I guess so."

"Don't sound so enthusiastic," he said with a chuckle. "After all, it was your idea." He handed her a smock to put over her top and took a moment to set up an easel. He leafed through a file of photos he kept for his students, took one out and placed it on a stand. "I figure we can start with something simple like a sunflower, and you can use that picture as a model."

Nadia blew out a long breath. "Okay, let's do this."

He showed her the best ways to hold the brush for different strokes, but ten minutes in, he could see the frustration on her beautiful face. "You're doing great, babe."

"For a damn kindergartner," she muttered.

Gavin roared with laughter. "It's your first time. Give yourself some grace."

She flicked a blob of paint on the canvas. "I can't do this."

"I see patience isn't your strong suit. And don't look at me like that," he said when she glared at him. "How about we try the pottery wheel? You said you wanted to do the *Ghost* scene. I'll even play music."

Her eyes lit up. "Ooh, 'Unchained Melody'?"

"Absolutely not."

Nadia folded her arms and pouted. "You have to play the song, Gavin."

"Stop pouting," he said with amusement. He dug out his phone, then synced it to the speakers he'd installed. Michaela had turned him on to the violin duo, Black Violin and he found their orchestral sound helped his creativity, just as she'd said. The first strains of "Dirty Orchestra" filled the room.

Nadia angled her head. "Okay, okay. I can get with this."

"Come here, baby." Gavin directed her to the stool in front of his pottery wheel, then sat on another one behind her. Because of their height differences, he didn't have any problems seeing the wheel. He centered a lump of clay, then added a little water using a sponge. "Give me your hands." He placed her hands around the clay and covered them with his.

She giggled. "It's cold. What are we making?"

"A bowl."

"Sounds simple, but I know it's not. I watched a few videos yesterday and some of what happened was not pretty. All I can see is the same thing happening to me."

"Nope. We're doing this together." He set the wheel in motion, using the sponge and their hands to mold and shape the outer walls.

"I'm doing it," she said excitedly. "This is so cool. I like your hands on mine."

"Behave."

"What? I'm talking about pottery."

"Uh huh." Sitting behind her this way with her body squirming against his was testing his control. Each time she got excited, her round ass bumped his growing erection, tempting him to create another work of art that involved her bent over his worktable or against any one of the four walls. Refocusing on the task, he continued using their hands and the sponge on top until it was the perfect height. "Okay, give me your index and middle fingers on your dominant hand."

"Sounds a little kinky, but okay."

"Nadia, you're about two seconds from not finishing this bowl."

"Fine." She gyrated her hips against him, and he groaned. "We'll finish the bowl, then each other."

"How the hell am I supposed to concentrate when you say stuff like that?"

She angled her head and kissed his cheek, then faced forward again. "I would say I'm sorry, but we said we'd always be honest with each other."

"Yeah, but can we table the honesty for the next five minutes?"

"Sure."

"Hold your fingers steady in the same position." He gently, steadily, and slowly eased them back toward the outer edge, being careful to keep his movements even and adding more water as needed to keep the clay wet.

"I can't believe it. It really looks like a bowl."

"Carefully lift your fingers and I'll finish." He continued shaping and trimming it with his fingers and tools. "What do you think?" he asked when he finished.

"It's amazing. I can't believe I helped make a bowl. I have to send Brooklyn a picture."

Gavin stood and wiped his hands on a damp cloth. "It'll

need to dry for a few days before firing it in the kiln. In the meantime," he said, nuzzling her neck, "I think there's something else we need to finish."

They washed and dried their hands, then he slowly stripped them both and donned a condom. "I'm not sure where I want you first, the table or the wall."

She peered at him through lowered lids and gave him a sultry smile. "I'm partial to the wall, but we can do both."

"I can get with that." He lifted her in his arms, carried her over to the wall and entered her with one long thrust. They both moaned. "Get ready to ride."

Nadia wrapped her arms around his neck and locked her legs around his back as he set a hard, driving rhythm. "*Yesss*, right there."

She arched and writhed against him as he pumped faster, delving deeper with each thrust, giving her everything she asked for. The sounds of ecstasy spilling from her mouth sent his desire soaring straight through the roof. He gasped as her feminine muscles clutched him tighter. No other woman came close to making him feel the way she did and he wanted to stay inside of her forever. "You feel so good," he murmured, his thrusts going deeper and faster. He could feel her body trembling and knew she was close. He wanted them to come together. Gavin planted his feet and drove into her. "Come with me, baby." Her nails dug into his chest and shoulders, and their blended cries echoed throughout the room.

Abruptly, Nadia let out a high-pitched scream as she climaxed all around him, her feminine muscles clenching him tight.

He gripped her hips and growled hoarsely when an explosive orgasm ripped through him with a force that stole his breath and left his entire body shaking. He held her tightly as they both shuddered with the aftershocks. He adjusted her in his arms and rested his forehead against hers.

"I love you, Gavin," she whispered breathlessly.

"I love you, too. Forever."

EPILOGUE

One year later.

"Ladies and gentlemen, I present to you Mr. and Mrs. Gavin Black!" Loud applause broke out all over the room.

Gavin escorted Nadia into the gallery that had been transformed for their wedding reception. They'd agreed that it was only fitting to hold it here, since this was where they first began falling in love.

"I'm so happy, I could scream," Nadia said, a huge grin on her face.

"Oh, Mrs. Black, you'll definitely be doing some screaming later. I guarantee it."

She swatted him on the arm. "Behave."

"Believe me, I'll be on my very best behavior. What do think about a quickie in my studio? With everybody being busy with all the food and drinks, no one will miss us." She didn't say anything, but started nibbling on her bottom lip, a sure sign she was thinking about it.

"Congratulations, big brother," Micah said, joining them.

"Thanks." They shared a one-arm hug and he said softly, "Your timing is lousy."

He chuckled. "I figured I'd rescue you from doing something that might get you into trouble, especially with Mom looking over here. You can sneak out with your bride later."

Gavin grunted. He glanced across the room where both mothers were chatting like old friends and smiling at them. He'd met Nadia's parents when they flew to Seattle last year and found them to be as wonderful as their daughter. Since the engagement, his mother had been more animated, more like her old self, and had even began painting again. Emotion filled his heart.

Micah turned to Nadia. "You're as beautiful as ever, Nadia, and I think I'm going to enjoy having a sister."

"Thanks. I've always wanted a brother. I'm going to make sure you're doing right by all the lovely ladies," she added sweetly.

"On second thought…"

Gavin and Nadia laughed as he hurried off. He said, "Now, where were we? Oh, I know. I was trying to convince you to join me in my studio for a few minutes."

"Stop trying to tempt me."

"You two look like you need a few private moments," her friend Brooklyn said, smiling. "How long do you need—fifteen, twenty minutes? I can run interference."

"Go away, Brooklyn," Nadia said. "Always trying to start trouble," she muttered.

"Oh, girl, hush. Go on give that man a little sumthin' sumthin' to hold him over until tonight. I did with Vince."

Gavin burst out laughing. "Brooklyn, fifteen minutes should do."

"I got you." She reached up and hugged him. "You'll always have a place in my heart for taking care of my girl, and for kicking Austin's trifling ass." He and her former boss were now locked up with their other friend. Because Austin had traveled across state lines, he'd ended up with some other added charges.

"I'd do anything for her," he said, stroking a finger down Nadia's cheek.

"I know." Brooklyn glanced down at her watch. "Okay. Go."

He grabbed Nadia by the hand, strode purposefully to his studio and locked the door. He gathered the fabric of her dress and pushed it up around her waist. Moving her panties to the side, he slid two fingers inside of her.

"Gavin," she said, laughing, "we can't just up and *ohhh*."

"Yeah, baby, we can." He dropped his pants, lifted her in his arms and drove into her with one deep thrust. "You are my heart."

"And you're mine."

Gavin had found the one who he could entrust his heart. The one who'd become his peace, his love, his everything.

ONCE UPON A MURDER SERIES

DEAR READER

Dear Reader ~

I'm always excited to be part of an anthology with my author sisters, and I hope you enjoyed Gavin and Nadia's journey to finding love. I also hope you enjoyed the cameo appearances of some familiar friends. As always, I look forward to hearing your thoughts.

Love & Blessings!
Sheryl
sheryllister@gmail.com
www.sheryllister.com

ABOUT THE AUTHOR

Sheryl Lister is a multi-award winning author who writes sweet, sensual contemporary romance featuring intelligent and slightly flawed characters who always find love. She is a former pediatric occupational therapist with over twenty years of experience and often says she "played" for a living. A California native, Sheryl is a wife, mother of three daughters and a son-in-love, and grandmother to two special boys. When she's not writing, Sheryl can be found on a date with her husband or in the kitchen creating appetizers. For more information, visit her website at www.sheryllister.com.

ALSO BY SHERYL LISTER

Just To Be With You

All OfMe

It's Only You

Be Mine For Christmas (Unwrapping The Holidays Anthology)

Tender Kisses (The Grays of Los Angeles #1)

Places In My Heart (The Grays of Los Angeles #2)

Giving My All To You (The Grays of Los Angeles #3)

A Touch Of Love (The Grays of Los Angeles #4)

Still Loving You (The Grays of Los Angeles #5)

His Los Angeles Surprise (Millionaire Moguls)

A Love Of My Own (The Hunters Of Sacramento #1)

Sweet Love (The Hunters Of Sacramento #2)

Spark Of Desire (The Hunters Of Sacramento #3)

Designed By Love (The Hunters Of Sacramento #4)

OTHER TITLES

Made To Love You

It's You That I Need

Perfect Chemistry

Embracing Forever (Once Upon A Bridesmaid #3)

Love's Serenade (Decades: A Journey Of African American Romance #3)

Sweet Summer Days (Grays Family & Friends)

The Reluctant Bid (Distinguished Gentlemen)

Closer To You

Her Passionate Promise (Women of Park Manor)

Love's Sweet Kiss (Sassy Seasoned Sisters #1)

Never Letting Go (Carnivale Chronicles)

Embracing Ever After (Once Upon a Baby #1)

Do Me (Irresistible Husband)

Five Midnight Moments (New Year Bae-Solutions)

Tempting Hunter (Once Upon A Funeral #4)

Love's Sweet Surrender (Sassy Seasoned Sisters #2)

Five Mistletoe Moments (Baes of Christmas)

A Table for Two (Firefly Lake #1)

Choose Me (Irresistible Husband)

Mr. Right Now (Baes of Juneteenth)

A Perfect Pairing (Firefly Lake #2)

No Reservations

Taste The Smoke

www.ingramcontent.com/pod-product-compliance
Lightning Source LLC
Chambersburg PA
CBHW030236180626
46810CB00008B/3151
* 9 7 8 1 7 3 7 3 3 0 1 6 5 *